What could make him nervous, such a powerful man asking a favor of a mere scullery maid?

"Go ahead," she prodded, hoping he didn't mind.

"My request is unorthodox. . ."

There was that word again. Apparently it was quite popular with the upper classes. She resolved to find out what it meant.

". . .and I pray you won't be offended, but you see, I'm in quite a pinch and I really need your help."

"My help? But I ain't nothin' but a maid, and the lowest maid at that. What could I possibly do for ya?"

"Something I hope you will find easy." He took in another breath. "Miss Hanham, will you marry me?"

TAMELA HANCOCK MURRAY is an award-winning, bestselling author living in northern Virginia. She and her husband of twenty-five years are blessed with two daughters. When not spending time with friends and family, Tamela enjoys writing stories of faith, hope, and love. Tamela also loves hearing from her fans! Check out her Web site at www.tamelahancockmurray.com

Books by Tamela Hancock Murray

The Master's Match

Tamela Hancock Murray

Heartsong Presents

*With special thanks to my parents, Herman and Ann Hancock.
You both have always given me your love and support.*

A note from the Author:
*I love to hear from my readers! You may correspond with
me by writing:*

Tamela Hancock Murray
Author Relations
PO Box 721
Uhrichsville, OH 44683

ISBN 978-1-60260-517-6

THE MASTER'S MATCH

All scripture quotations are taken from the King James Version of the
Bible.

All the characters and events in this book are fictitious. Any resemblance
to actual persons, living or dead, or to actual events is purely coincidental.

*Our mission is to publish and distribute inspirational products offering
exceptional value and biblical encouragement to the masses.*

PRINTED IN THE U.S.A.

prologue

Providence, Rhode Island
1838

Ten-year-old Becca Hanham could not go home until she sold enough lucifers to buy bread. She pulled a ragged shawl around her tiny shoulders, but the motion did little to ward off the cold of a December evening in Providence. Standing by the tavern, she heard piano music, laughter, and singing from within. No wonder each night Father escaped to the light and warmth of such a place. At home Mother always looked sad, and Becca's brothers and sisters filled their cramped rented rooms with yelling and crying. Still, Becca yearned to go back. Whistling wind bit her bare legs.

She peered down the familiar street of Providence, hoping for customers. At the first cross street, a tall man wearing a stylish hat and unblemished outer coat walked alongside a woman donned in a fur-trimmed cape. Looking into each other's eyes, they laughed and talked as they approached.

What would it be like to be so happy? Becca wondered.

Soon the couple drew close enough to hear her. "Lucifers, sir?" Her hand shivered as she held the matches out to him.

He shook his head.

Knowing better than to pose her question to the lady, Becca set her gaze on the street and returned the lucifers to the small reed basket hanging from the crook of her arm.

"The poor little thing," she heard the woman mutter as they kept strolling. "Oh, Thomas, can't you buy some to help her? Your servants tend many fireplaces at your estate."

"You are too kindhearted, Elizabeth. If I bought goods from every street urchin, I'd soon be living alongside them. And so would you, after we're wed. You wouldn't want that, would you?" Even his thick topcoat didn't hide a shudder.

The woman glimpsed back at Becca. "No, I suppose not."

The first time Becca had heard similar observations, she felt a bite deeper than the cold, but since then she had grown too resilient to let such comments bother her. Why should anyone want to change places with her? A quick look at her reflection in a dark window confirmed that a washed face and clean clothes couldn't conceal her ragamuffin status.

Another couple, this time appearing to be mother and son, approached. Becca held out her wares and offered them for sale, but they kept their gazes from touching her.

The little girl fought discouragement. *If I can sell but a few more, I'll have enough money. Oh, it is so cold! Father in heaven, please send me a buyer soon.* She peered at the matches in her basket. If only there were a fireplace with blazing logs nearby. Then she could keep warm. But the nearest fireplace burned in the tavern, and children weren't welcome there. Thoughts of lighting a lucifer on a cobblestone visited her, but such a tiny flame wouldn't keep her warm long. Why, it would hardly warm her at all. How many times had Mother told her not to light matches since any she used would eat into their profit?

So cold. So cold.

With no one in sight, she couldn't resist. She had to light one. Kneeling to reach the cobblestone, she struck it hard against the surface, inhaling the strong odor of sulfur. How terrible hell must be if the doomed must smell sulfur forever. She shook. Still, the warmth against her palms helped, if only for a moment. She let the stick burn as long as she could before dropping it. Then there was no light and no warmth.

Dismal thoughts of the condemned left as she spotted a young man, just in his teens, rushing up the street toward her.

His face looked the way she imagined young David's in the Bible—the courageous youth who beat a giant with a mere sling. Mother described him as comely. To Becca's eyes, that adjective fit the approaching figure. Her gaze took in his mode of dress. A stylish overcoat and fine leather boots told her he wasn't a servant, and he was too young to worry about keeping a fire lit. Discouragement visited. He wouldn't buy any lucifers. Still, she had to try.

He had almost passed her before she summoned the courage ask, "Lucifers, sir?"

To her shock, he stopped. Looking down at her, his brown eyes not only caught her gaze but filled with compassion. He nodded. "It's terribly cold tonight. A girl like you shouldn't be out."

A blush of embarrassment warmed her face but gave her no comfort. "My family needs to eat, young master."

"Of course. Well, we have lots of fireplaces at my house. Cook will be happy to see a new box of lucifers."

"A whole box, sir?" She tried not to gasp with happiness.

"Yes." He extended his gloved hand. "May I have the lucifers, please?"

Wary, she nodded and handed them to him, then watched him place the container in his coat pocket. She prayed she hadn't been duped, that as a joke he would run off with her wares without paying. If that happened, Father would whip her for sure. She swallowed.

He remained in place and took off a black leather glove. She couldn't help but wish she had gloves to cover her bare fingers. "Hold out your hands, please."

She extended one hand.

He smiled. "No, both. If you will."

"Both?" Yet she complied.

He reached into another pocket and withdrew a number of coins, then placed them in her open palms.

She gasped, noting most were ten-cent coins. Never had she been so grateful to see an engraving of Lady Liberty with a star for each of the thirteen original colonies surrounding her image. "But this is too much, sir."

He slid his fine glove back over his hand. "Perhaps you might buy a pair of mittens."

She would never be permitted to spend money on herself but didn't want to point out the fact. "Really, sir, I must charge only what's fair."

"I don't want any of it back. Please. Keep the money in the name of Christian charity."

Christian charity wasn't unknown to her, but such generosity was, even in the name of Christ. She tried not to gasp. "Are—are ya sure?"

"I've never been more certain of anything."

She'd never held so much money in her life. "Thank you, sir. Thank you from the bottom of my heart." Clutching the money, she hurried to buy the bread so she could rush home and warm her toes by the fire.

"Lord, I know that stranger didn't need so many lucifers. He bought them out of mercy. I didn't know there could be so much kindness—at least not for me," she muttered. "I'm so glad he belongs to Thee. Please, keep him in Thy protection forever."

one

1848

"How much longer will that triflin' Abby girl be gone? I'm hungry." Father's voice bellowed from the room he shared with his wife and the babies.

Up to her elbows in dishwater, Becca shuddered. She recalled her days as the family's match girl and Father's wrath if she didn't sell enough lucifers to keep the family fed. If only he could get his job back at the factory, but he loved the bottle more than any work, and even the most patient boss couldn't afford her father's drunkenness and absences. The brother who did manage to keep a factory job had wed, so his earnings supported his wife and their new baby girl.

What little income their household earned came from sporadic odd jobs she and her younger siblings could pick up now and again. Two older sisters had married as quickly as they could to escape and now had their own homes to manage. In the meantime Becca, now the oldest of the remaining siblings, spent her waking hours helping Mother with Becca's brothers and sisters. One could almost set the calendar by the arrival of a new Hanham baby each year. With so many mouths to feed, they were forced to squeeze the most out of every cent.

Wiping a dish without setting her mind to the task, she recalled that bitter evening so many years ago. Each day since then she had prayed for the safety of the young man who had bought lights from her when she was at her most desperate point. If he hadn't shown her such mercy, she wondered how long she would have suffered in the unusually bitter and miserably cold night.

"Becca!" Father's voice punctured the air as he entered the front room that served as the kitchen and parlor.

She let the semiclean dish fall back into the water and turned halfway toward him. "Yea, Father?"

"Look at me when I speak to ya." A tall figure, he appeared imposing even when he wasn't in a foul mood.

"Yes, Father." Without stopping to swipe water from her hands, she faced him.

"Where is that Abby girl?" He sat at the table, the burden of his weight causing the old pine chair, most of its varnish long worn off, to creak.

"Little Abby? I'm sure she's still out sellin' lucifers, Father." Becca looked outside. "It's still mornin'. She has hours left. Oftentimes I had to sell well into the night, remember?"

He grunted.

"I just hope she doesn't have to stay out too long today. This January weather chills to the bone."

"I doubt she'll stay out all night like you did," Father observed. "She's a shirker, that's what she is. Ya always brought in enough fer us." He eyed a nearby pitcher. "Pour me some ale now."

She wanted to defend little Abby but knew that argument would do more harm than good and increase Father's ill temper. Instead she remained agreeable and picked up the pitcher. "Yea, Father."

Poor Abby. Memories of how difficult being a match girl was flooded her, bringing her angst. As soon as Father swigged the portion of ale Becca poured, she returned to her dishes. At least the numbing drink would keep him occupied and quiet for a few dear moments.

The next instant, Mother came back from errands, a tired expression on her face. When she entered, a blast of cold air followed her through the open door.

"Shut the door, woman," Father said. "It's cold enough in here as it is."

Becca couldn't argue that. In winter the house never felt warm enough.

"I'm sorry."

Becca looked at the reed basket Mother used for groceries and realized it held precious little.

"Where's the food?" Father asked. "Seems like ya didn't hardly bring us nothin'."

Setting the basket on the table, Mother apologized in a small voice. "I bought what I could with the pennies I had. Mr. Sloane says he won't give us no more credit. We have to pay up our bill."

Father snarled and set down his mug with enough force to bang against the table. "Is that so? Why, I oughta go right there and give 'im some o' this, I should." He pounded his left fist into his open right palm.

Mother rushed to his side and placed a restricting hand on his shoulder. "Please don't. Not now. Especially not now with the new baby on the way."

Though the announcement didn't come as a surprise, Becca suppressed a groan. She chastised herself for her feelings, but a new life would make things even harder for the family. "A—another baby? But Bennie is only three months old."

"Shut yer mouth, girl. A new baby's a blessin', I tell you, if it's a boy." Father puffed up his chest. "Soon the children I sire will be enough to fill all of Providence. I'm sure this new baby will be a healthy boy."

Thoughts of two lost siblings sent a wave of sadness through Becca. Obadiah had lived only a day after his birth. A passive little thing, he'd withered away and died. Why, they did not know. Five years ago another little boy, Manny, had been run over and killed by a horse when he was crossing the street trying to reach a customer wanting a newspaper. They lived in a dangerous world, and only cautious children with strong constitutions survived to adulthood. Becca prayed the new life in Mother's womb was already endowed by God with both of those traits.

"A baby's a blessin' whether a boy or girl." Mother frowned. "But I hate bringin' a new life into a place where there ain't enough money to pay fer food. What will we do?"

"I know what we can do." Father set his gaze on his daughter. "Becca, ye're a good worker. It's past time fer ya to get a job that pays a wage."

Mother paled. "But what will I do? I need Becca here to help me."

"Enough, woman. Ya don't need to be such a sloth. Time for ya to take on more work so we can feed this family." Pride filled his voice. "Yea, it's a good thing for a man to sire a brood o' twenty and countin'."

Mother remained at Father's side but turned her face to Becca. Wide eyes and a distressed line of her mouth told her she wanted help convincing Father that their daughter shouldn't get a job.

A fortifying breath gave Becca courage. "Father, I want to stay here and tend to me brothers and sisters."

"Enough of that. If ya don't want to work in town, ya can always wed. At least then with ya married and out of the house, there'll be one less mouth to feed. Just think o' yer older sisters and brothers, all with husbands and wives of their own now. And with Deb havin' a little one o' her own soon, I'll be a grandfather again. Six and countin'. Why don't ya do me proud, too?" Father rubbed salt-and-pepper stubble on his chin and rocked his chair back against the wall. "Ya know, I've seen how Micah Judd looks at ya. Maybe the two o' ya could make a go of it."

The image of a rotund, unkempt boy who couldn't utter a thought without cursing came to mind. "That foul oaf?"

How Father managed to look offended, she didn't know. "He ain't so bad now. What's the matter? Think ya can do better—mebbe get a wealthy gentleman?" His laugh sounded ugly.

"You might not believe me, but money ain't me goal."

"And that's a good thing, too, since there ain't no money 'round this part o' town." Father chortled.

Becca remained serious, facing her father as she leaned against the counter. "I don't fancy Micah because he's not a godly man. And I don't love him."

"Love him?" Father's chuckle had no mirth. "There's more to marriage than love." He looked to Mother for confirmation. "Ain't that right, woman?"

"Love is a nice thing to have. That's why I'm still here." Mother's quiet voice matched her meekness as she stared at the tabletop.

"Is that right? I don't believe it. No, ye're here because I kept ya and yer kids fed and clothed all these years." Father folded his arms and cleared his throat.

Mother surveyed her cotton dress, thin with wear and mended more than once, before her gaze shot up to meet his. "We started out in love. Remember those days?" Hurt mixed with wistfulness colored her voice.

"Sure I do." His voice was devoid of emotion as he dismissed his wife and turned to his daughter. "Now, girl, ya can make a good life with Micah. No doubt about it."

Queasiness stabbed at her gut. "No, Father. I'll find me a job."

"So ye're serious?" Mother's eyebrows rose, and her mouth slackened in alarm. "Where?"

"I don't know, Mother." How could she know? She hadn't considered the possibility until moments ago. "I—I ain't got no skills, 'cept the ones I learned at yer knee."

"Yea, ya know how to run a household better than anyone

else I know," she agreed. "Surpassin' even meself, I'd say."

"There's no better place to use what ya learned here than in a position as a wife." Father shrugged. "But if ya can find a job, suit yerself. That will be more money to line me pocket. Mebbe Mr. Whittaker would hire ya at the tavern. I could put in a good word fer ya."

Becca imagined if she took such a position she'd be ogled and prodded by drunken men, young and old alike. Not to mention Father would expect her to pour him ale for free when the owner wasn't watching. "I–I'd rather work somewhere else."

He scowled. "Where, Miss High Horse? Like ya said yerself, ya ain't got no trainin' fer a good job."

"Maybe one of the factories will take me."

Mother pursed her lips. "No doubt they will, a hard worker like you. But ya know from yer brother's experience that the hours are long and the work can be dangerous."

"The pay is good," Father said.

"Yea, but I think ye'd be happier doin' somethin' else." Mother brightened. "I know. Ye're wonderful with yer brothers and sisters. Mebbe ya can be a nanny for some upper-crust folks."

"That's it! Why, I don't mind helpin' ya here around the house. So why should I mind helpin' out some society woman? I'd think she'd have less children than we have runnin' around here." Becca spoke faster as her excitement increased. "Yea, I think I could do that." Without considering the consequences, she took off her tired apron, threw it over a kitchen chair, and headed to the tiny room she shared in discomfort with eight sisters.

Mother followed her. "What are ya doin'?"

"I'm takin' ya up on yer suggestion, that's all. If I'm a-thinkin' I'll get me a job, I'd better look me best. So I'm washin' me face and hands." A quick lean toward the mirror told her she looked presentable enough, even under close scrutiny. Behind her, she caught Mother's reflection. The graying woman's shoulders stooped more than usual, making her seem even older than her forty years. Any trace of happiness had vanished from her face and demeanor. Sighing, Mother crossed her hands over her chest. She looked at the straw-stuffed mattresses on the floor as though she considered sitting on one but seemed to think better of it and remained standing.

Becca didn't turn around. Instead she twisted her coffee-colored hair into a flattering upward style as she consoled her parent, leaving a few ringlets to fall loose around her face. "Don't be sad, Mother. Think of this as a new adventure. Fer me, fer all of us. Maybe the whole Hanham clan will be better off because I went and worked fer some society folks." Becca retrieved her best dress—the one she wasn't wearing at present—out of the oak wardrobe that Grandfather had made for Mother on the occasion of her wedding. The old and simple garment was no longer considered fashionable, but it would have to do. She slipped off her old dress and slid the clean cotton frock over her petticoats, grateful that she made a point of keeping one step ahead in the ongoing battle against mounds of dirty clothes.

"But I didn't think ye'd be taking action so soon," Mother protested to the point she whined.

Unaccustomed to her mother complaining, Becca winced. "I'm sorry, but I can't marry Micah, and if I don't do somethin' to earn money quicklike, Father will have us at the altar before we can take in a breath." She touched her mother's shoulder. "Ya don't blame me fer not wantin' to hitch meself to Micah, do ya? Please say ya don't blame me."

"I don't. I want someone better than Micah for ya, too, even if he does have a good position at the silver factory. But a job fer me Becca now? I thought we was just talkin' before."

One of Becca's brothers, Samuel, ran in and put his face

in his mother's skirts. Concerned about his own problems, the boy didn't notice he had interrupted a critical exchange between his mother and sister. "They won't wet me pway wif 'em," the little fellow wailed.

Both women knew "they" referred to his older siblings and assorted neighborhood children. Mother stroked his curly blond locks. "Tell yer brothers and sisters I said to let ya play with 'em or I'll make 'em come in the rest of the day. Run along now."

He lifted his face, smiled, and nodded. "I'll tell 'em."

Mother watched him run out. "Ah, to be young. Ever'thin's right with the world in a minute."

"If you're a boy around here, that's so." Becca sighed. "At least Father let Laban choose his own wife."

"Yea, but who can object to Lizzie?"

The image of a green-eyed beauty popped into her head. Lizzie made Laban happy. What more could anyone want? "She's one of my favorites, she is. I wish she had a brother older than ten," Becca ventured in half jest.

Mother's laugh brightened the room. "There's plenty o' crop around here. Maybe one of the other fellas caught yer eye? Ye're pretty enough to have any boy around. Peter, maybe?"

He appealed to Becca more than Father's choice of Micah, but not enough to wed. "No, Mother. There ain't nobody I want. At least nobody I've seen around here. I'd rather be an old maid than be unhappy in marriage."

Mother gasped. "An old maid! Ya don't mean it!"

"I do. I won't marry someone I don't love. You love Father, and your marriage is hard enough."

Mother looked at the floor. "I can't deny it."

"I'll do as Father says and get me a job. Today is as good a day as any to get started." She peered outside the window to eye the midmorning sun cutting the rising fog over the

Providence River. "It's early yet. I have the whole day ahead o' me. I 'spect I'll have a job by noon." She took her coat out of the wardrobe.

"That wrap looks mighty worn. If I'da known you'd be lookin' fer work, I'da sewn ya a new one."

Becca fought the impulse to ask Mother how, considering they lacked for grocery money and probably were behind on rent, too. A new coat would be an ambitious sewing project requiring much fabric. Instead Becca whipped on the gray garment she already owned and buttoned it to the top. "This coat has come in good, and it's still more than warm enough to fight the Narragansett winds. At least it don't usually get as chilly here as Aunt Hilda says it gets in the Berkshires."

"We can thank the good Lord for that." Mother paused, and her eyes grew misty. "I don't want ya to go. Let me speak with yer father. I can talk some sense into him."

Becca had seen her mother's pleas for any favor ignored too many times by her father to believe such a brag. "I knows ya need help, Mother, but Mary can take over some of my load. And her chores can go to Sissy. And Naomi's already doin' more than her share."

"I can't argue none of that." Tears flowing from her mother's eyes betrayed her sense of helplessness.

Becca embraced her mother. "Aw, it ain't as bad as all that. In a way Father's right. It's time I made my way in the world. And don't worry. I ain't goin' far. I'll try to work close enough that I can come home ever' night."

"I ain't sure about that. Babies wake up in the night, ya know, and their mothers want the nanny to tend to 'em. Don't count on seein' much of us if ya get a job as a nanny." Mother choked but composed herself enough to offer Becca a close-lipped half smile. "Then you'd best take your other dress and personal necessities along with ya."

Becca packed as her mother suggested, then donned a

woolen bonnet before giving her mother one last embrace. "I'll be fine. Don't ya worry, now."

"I hope so. Ya know, there's been talk of bank robbers strikin' in the better parts of town. I want ya to stay safe, ya hear?"

"Oh, Mother. What would a bank robber want with me? I don't have nothin' of value on my person, and I ain't got no reason to go near a bank. Ya worry too much." She picked up a cloth bag she had embroidered for herself, a small luxury she felt added a bit of fashion to her plain style of dress.

"Mebbe I do. I'll try not to so much." Mother squeezed her one last time before letting her go. She wouldn't let her gaze meet her daughter's. "I–I'd better get to my dustin'. And there's lunch to think about. Another burden fer me, now that ya won't be here."

"Remember, there are sisters behind me to take me place. Why, ya won't miss me a'tall."

Mother sniffled.

Forcing herself to leave her mother behind, Becca went through the front room. Her father hadn't moved from the table.

He looked her over and then eyed the satchel. "Goin' outside, eh? What's that ya got there?"

"My clothin'. I might not be able to come back ever' night. But I promised Mother I'll try."

"So you're really goin' to get a job at some rich woman's house." He let out a grunt. "I wish ya luck." His tone indicated he thought her chances were as good as walking a city block without encountering horse manure.

She decided to remain cheerful. "Thank ya, Father."

"Ya just be sure to bring yer money to me. Ya got yer family to feed. Ya don't need to buy perfume and dresses and hats fer yerself."

She'd never been free with what little money she ever

earned—not even the hands full of change from that young man so long ago. Why Father gave her such admonition, she didn't know. "Yea, Father."

"And another thing before ya go."

She looked at him with more hope than she meant. Perhaps he would offer a few kind words to her before she left. Maybe even an embrace. "Yea, Father?"

"Pour me another portion o' ale."

※

Nash Abercrombie sat at the desk in his study, mulling over a stack of correspondence in need of urgent tending. He'd been abroad, and the number of papers in the pile overwhelmed him. Though Nash's official period of mourning for his father, Timothy Abercrombie, had slipped away in a sad blur, many of the letters and notices concerned matters regarding the estate. Addressing them felt painful. Not a day passed when Nash didn't grieve over his loss. He had always felt badly enough that he never knew his mother, but why did his father have to be taken away much too early—and in Nash's absence when he couldn't be at his deathbed to tell him good-bye? Father and son knew they loved each other, but Nash wished he could have told him one last time on this side of heaven. His father had been manly, yet gentle and kind with a ready laugh and a God-fearing spirit. The world suffered more without him.

His faithful old butler knocked.

"Yes?" Nash answered.

"Pardon me, sir," Harrod said. "Cook asks if you would like her to send Jack to the Providence Arcade for lobster. She suggests it for dinner tonight."

He smiled. "The thought is kind of her, but really, I am dining alone and don't require such extravagance."

"Cook knows lobster is your favorite, and she wants to celebrate your arrival. We all celebrate your arrival, sir."

The notion of such a delicacy tempted him, but the reality of eating alone, along with the price of lobster in winter, left him without an appetite. God had provided him with more than enough wealth, but squandering money seemed unwise from both a spiritual and practical standpoint. "Perhaps I can indulge in lobster this spring when I can host a proper dinner party. Tell her I appreciate her consideration, but tonight I'd love some of her delicious vegetable soup and herb bread. And a bit of cheese, if she has it on hand."

"She'll be disappointed, but I commend you on your frugal ways. Your father would be proud, sir."

Nash dismissed Harrod and swallowed a lump in his throat as the old servant took his leave. Harrod had been Father's valet and butler and now served Nash in the same capacity. Harrod's good opinion meant something to him.

Tapping his ivory stylus on the top of the desk, he couldn't help but think of Hazel Caldwell. In her eyes a modest soup would hardly be considered an adequate first course for a light luncheon. In his mind he could hear her chastising him for dining as a pauper would. He would hate to see the bills Hazel's future husband would be forced to pay.

He prayed someone would talk sense into Hazel so she wouldn't hold on to the dream of their marriage. He might not have told Papa he loved him before he died, but Nash did tell him his desire was not to wed Hazel, no matter how prestigious and important her family name and connections. Nash and the Abercrombie wealth were nothing more than a means to her social ends. Judging from the way she treated him—never taking an interest in him as a person and every discussion involving extravagance—her love for him could be contained in the tip of a hummingbird's beak.

He set down his stylus and rested his face in his open hands, thinking. Nash was no fool and knew about loveless matches in his circle. All would be well and proper on the surface. Wives chosen for beauty, prestige, or fortune—or some combination thereof—fulfilled their duty by providing heirs as soon as was proper after the wedding day. Then they took consolation in discreet love affairs, profligate spending, or both. Meanwhile the husbands took a mistress—or two. The idea of such an unbiblical arrangement sickened him, and never would his father have asked Nash to live his life in such a way.

Of course some of his friends and acquaintances had found love within their marriages. He wanted to be among their number. And that meant convincing Hazel that she would make a better match with someone else.

He smiled, knowing the expression held no joy. *She needs someone else indeed. Someone who can love her.*

He put his hands together in prayer. "Lord, give me the strength and courage to follow Thy will and my heart."

two

Cloth satchel stuffed with everything she owned in the world on her arm, Becca set out with a determined step. The wealthy people's houses were up the hill, and up the hill she planned to go.

Frigid wind rubbed at her cheeks, but she tried not to think about the cold. She hadn't told her mother a fib about the warmth of her coat. As long as she kept walking, she stayed passably comfortable except where the coat didn't quite cover her skin. She'd worn the wrap several years, and the sleeves fell a bit short. But the mittens Mother knitted for her this past Christmas warmed her hands, and remnants of rags stuffed in her boots shielded her feet where the soles were worn through.

As she walked into the wealthy part of town, the atmosphere and scenery changed. Boisterous crowds couldn't be heard, and leering men didn't loiter in this part of town. Ramshackle, unpainted dwellings gave way to fine homes where, judging from appearances, inhabitants lived in luxury—or at least comfort. Self-conscious from the occasional curious stare aimed her way, she tilted her chin upward to show she indeed belonged there. After all, she was on a mission. She had just as much right to be there as anyone else.

Though she had entered a neighborhood on Benefit Street where ladies could afford nannies, she kept walking. No house looked more welcoming than another, and no reason presented itself as to why she shouldn't start knocking on doors. She stalled out of nervousness, despite her attempts to appear otherwise.

"Lord, where do I go?"

Gray clouds drifted over the sky, taking with them the brittle warmth from the winter sun. The time to start her search in earnest had arrived. Reaching a corner, she read the post. WILLIAMS STREET.

She smoothed her skirt and hair. Straightening her shoulders, she strolled to the front of a well-maintained house with a pretty wooden door and knocked.

A butler answered and inspected her with a keen eye. "How dare you, girl. Don't you know the help goes to the back?" The door banged shut.

She had never entertained illusions about her importance in society's ranks—her rung on the ladder hovered near the bottom—but she hadn't expected to encounter such rudeness, especially from a servant. She lingered at the door and gathered her thoughts. *He called me "the help." Come to think of it, I sure am the help. At least I hope I will be by the end of the day.*

Within minutes she found herself at the back door. Temptation to report the butler's unpleasant manner visited her, but she dismissed it. Snitching on a servant as Samuel tattled on his siblings would gain her no respect. She widened her eyes and set her mouth in a slightly upturned bow so she wouldn't show she'd already been treated in an abrupt manner. She took off the mitten on her right hand and knocked.

"Ye're late!" The shrill voice whizzed into the air before the door opened!

"I'm late?"

By this time an obese woman wearing a white cotton bonnet and apron splattered with melted lard stood before her. "Oh, I thought ya were the delivery boy. Who are ya, and what da ya want wif us?"

Becca didn't think the cook would be much help, but

there was no reason to be rude—even though the butler had slammed the door in her face. "I'd like to speak with the mistress of the house, please."

"Ya would, would ya?" The woman eyed her. "Concernin' what?"

"I'd like a job. As a nanny."

The woman laughed so loudly Becca jumped back. "There ain't no need for a nanny here. Mistress is nearly sixty, and she lives alone wif nuffin' but us servants. Off with ya now. I've work to do."

"But—but surely there must be someone in one of these houses nearby needin' a nanny."

"How do ya expect me ta know such a thing? I come here to work, not gossip. Off with ya, I say." The woman banged the door shut in Becca's face.

Not about to let the grumpy cook get the best of her, Becca tried one house after another, trekking from one street to the next. Between each unsuccessful encounter, she watched the weather, hoping she could take shelter should snow start to fall.

At the seventeenth house, a pretty young maid answered. "A nanny? Why, yes, we're looking for a nanny. Mr. and Mrs. Gill are the parents of three girls, ages two, four, and five. And we are expecting a new arrival later this year."

Becca almost jumped up and down with glee. "That sounds wonderful."

The maid's eyebrows rose. "Really? You'd be surprised how many girls run away nearly screaming at the thought of three small charges and a new infant." She gave Becca a knowing grin. "I think she'll see you."

Becca's heart beat with anticipation as she followed the maid. Their little family sounded easy to tend in comparison to caring for her many siblings at home.

The maid escorted her into a small sitting room upstairs. On the way she couldn't help but drink in the sight of life-sized portraits painted in oils, ornate furnishings, and elaborate draperies. She imagined even a small table cost more than her family earned in a year. What would it be like to work in such a fine residence? She hoped to find out.

The sitting room proved simpler, but the woman did not. Donned in a morning dress that would have suited most people for church, she looked down her nose at Becca from her position on a settee and did not offer her a seat despite the availability of two chairs. "You don't look like a nanny."

"What does a nanny look like?"

"I don't know." The woman shifted in her seat, clearly taken aback that Becca had posed a question she couldn't answer without some thought. "More educated, I suppose. How much schooling have you had?"

"Hard to say, ma'am. Mother taught me how to read, write, and cipher numbers. She says I catch on real fast."

"I see. So you haven't had many advantages in life." Her tone reminded Becca of the long icicles hanging off the woman's front awning.

Becca's mouth fell open, embarrassing her. "How'd ya know?"

"I catch on real fast myself." The woman's slight smile told Becca she fancied herself funny, but Becca felt the joke had been made at her expense. "So where is your letter of recommendation?"

"Letter of recommendation?"

"Yes. Surely you have references to approach me in such a manner."

"References?"

Mrs. Gill breathed out once before speaking. "People who can tell me you'll be a good nanny."

"Oh. Well, Mother told me that's what I should be. I've helped take care of me brothers and sisters ever since I can remember."

"And how many do you have?"

"Nineteen, with another one on the way."

The woman gasped. "I suppose I could count that as experience with children. What caused you to visit me looking for a job as a nanny?"

How could she answer such a strange question? Mrs. Gill's house had been next in line, that's all. Becca had a feeling such an answer wouldn't impress the formidable woman. Honesty appeared to be her best option. "Me father said if I don't marry, I have to work."

"Oh. Is that the only reason?"

She took in a breath. "The only reason I'm a-lookin', yes, ma'am."

"I see. And someone who knows your father knows me? One of my lower-ranking servants, perhaps?"

Tired of this line of questioning and its implied insults, Becca laid out the whole truth. "I don't think so. I just walked till I found a street with pretty houses and started knockin' on doors."

Mrs. Gill clutched at her throat. "My, but that is unorthodox."

Becca wasn't sure what that meant, but she thought it best to nod.

Her interviewer stiffened. "So you have no formal credentials, no experience, and you know no one other than your parents who can recommend you?"

"Nobody as rich as you are."

Becca thought she discerned the slightest hint of a genuine smile touching the woman's lips, but that instant soon passed. "Someone in my position cannot entrust anyone without references or formal experience with the care of my precious children. I require someone far more cultured." She called for the maid.

Becca wasn't sure what to say next, but she did know from talking to other girls in her neighborhood who'd been servants that no matter what, you had to seem grateful. "Thank you, ma'am."

The maid arrived before the words left Becca's lips. "Escort her out, Mindy. And don't bring anyone else to me without proper proof of worth, or you'll summarily be dismissed. I have better things to do than to waste my time."

The maid quaked. "Yes, ma'am."

"I'm sorry," Becca whispered to the maid as they went to the back door. "She must be a fright to work for."

"Good-bye." Despite her harsh tone, something in the maid's eyes told Becca she had guessed right.

Back outdoors, Becca's steps slowed in spite of the fact a light snow fell. Maybe Father's warnings had been true. Maybe she was too worthless to get any type of job. "Lord, what should I do?"

❧

"Don't bother to announce me, Harrod." Hazel's commanding voice floated three floors up to his private study from the front hall. He wished he'd had the foresight to stay in his downstairs study where he met with business associates. But it was too late to change now.

"Nash will see me any time."

Nash cringed at the prospect of seeing her, but he prepared himself by putting away his Bible and making sure his face looked pleasant when she entered. He heard the muffled voice of Harrod, no doubt objecting that Nash shouldn't be disturbed without notice, but he knew no amount of opposition from anyone would deter Hazel. Nash envisioned her tossing her hat, gloves, and wrap to Harrod in a dismissive way. Poor Harrod. He'd be getting a generous bonus for his birthday this year.

Soon Hazel breezed into the study. "Nash, why didn't you send word you're home? I had to hear it from Laurel's upstairs maid who heard it from your chambermaid."

"I'll have to tell my chambermaid not to gossip."

"Truly, Nash, you are such a jester." She flitted her hand in his direction. "Why are you alone up here in this lonely study, popular as you are? Now that your official period of mourning for your father is over, it's time to resume your social life. I hope you're planning a party to celebrate your homecoming."

"I hadn't given the notion much thought."

She stood erect, reminding him of a stern sea captain. "Have you no intention of offering me a seat?"

"Please sit down." He nodded to the only other chair in the room.

She let out a breath, which told Nash she had expected him to rise and escort her to the chair. His mood allowed for no such nicety.

"Now, as for the party," she said as she seated herself, "I must consult your cook to be sure we have a proper menu. We wouldn't want anyone to think I'm engaged to marry a poor man, now, would we?"

Marriage to Hazel. The thought made him shiver.

"Cold, dear?" Hazel asked. "No wonder, with how you never allow the servants to keep a decent fire going. It's winter, you know, and you have plenty of money to keep the house warm. Why, when I stepped in the hallway just now, I hardly noticed the difference between the outdoors and inside."

"I hadn't asked for a fire in the front rooms today since I wasn't expecting company."

"But what if someone of great power, prestige, and influence comes to call? Surely you wouldn't want an important person to suffer the indignities of cold."

"Anyone dropping in unannounced deserves what he gets." Nash grinned in hopes she would see the spoonful of levity in his remark, but her open mouth showed horror.

"How terrible! Laurel would never stand for such an inhospitable attitude."

"Mitchell Gill is to be commended for earning money faster than the rate at which your sister can spend it."

"She spends it to keep up appearances, and that's what we should do once we're wed." Hazel's nose lifted a bit as she sniffed.

Nash leaned back in his chair. "Keeping up appearances is costly and not good stewardship."

"You sound like the preacher. Wasn't that the topic of his sermon last week? I never said we wouldn't give a little to the church. At least enough to keep up our standing—worthy of our position as occupants of the Abercrombie family pew—and to assure our family proper treatment on each and every baptism, funeral, and wedding," Hazel countered. "And speaking of weddings, when shall we set our date?"

"I suggest that might occur after I make a formal proposal of marriage. And I have no intention of doing so."

Hazel waved her hand as if batting at a gnat. "Ever since we waltzed the night away at the Harris cotillion, everyone knew it was only a matter of time before we'd be wed."

Nash tightened his lips. Indeed, he had been enchanted by Hazel that one night—the night they met when she moved into Providence to live with her sister. She had looked especially beautiful and beguiling, and her charming conversation had kept him entertained all evening. For a few fleeting moments, he thought he might love her one day.

He had no idea that she would become so unpleasant and self-serving overnight.

Or that, desperate for a society match, she would latch on to him and never let go.

Perhaps he had been the one who beguiled her, although he had made no promises nor been anything but a gentleman. He wished he'd never seen her, for no matter how sour a disposition he displayed in her presence or how much he protested he had no plans to marry her, she and her sister seemed bound and determined that Hazel would become Mrs. Nash Abercrombie. Even his absence, during which he never wrote her, hadn't dampened her resolve. He had to stop her plans. But how?

"I must say," she prattled, "Laurel pesters me every hour on the hour about when we will be having our engagement party."

Nash could feel time closing in on him. The situation had become clear. There was no hope in putting her off.

"Everyone is so excited about our wedding. Have you spoken to your groomsmen yet?"

"No." He didn't want to speak to anyone.

"I believe I mentioned twelve groomsmen, but now the number has increased to fourteen. Laurel wants me to include two of our cousins as bridesmaids I hadn't considered since they were in her wedding. I know someone as powerful and popular as you can easily find fourteen groomsmen."

Nash didn't answer. Of course, by asking every woman they knew to be in her wedding, Hazel had eliminated them from considering Nash as a suitor. He suspected Laurel had mapped out the strategy and Hazel hadn't hesitated to go along with it.

"But enough wedding talk. Men are bored to tears with such things. At least that's what my brother-in-law tells me whenever Laurel and I start discussing it."

Nash didn't answer. He knew Gill's protests of boredom signaled to the women they should come to their senses, but they were too stubborn to take the hint. Nash had a feeling he wouldn't be bored listening to the woman he really wanted to marry speak about their wedding.

"About the wedding, Hazel. . ."

She arched an eyebrow. "Yes?"

"I had hoped by my lack of correspondence with you while I was away that you would have discerned my feelings.

However, I can see that I'll have to state my thoughts plainly." He paused. "It pains me that you continue to speak of the wedding. I have tried to tell you many times that I have no intention of going through with it. Why won't you listen?"

"Don't be ridiculous, Nash. Everyone knows we're planning to wed. You're just getting cold feet, that's all."

"I'm afraid it's more than cold feet, Hazel." Feeling pain at having to hurt her, Nash paused. "You are a fine woman in many ways, but I just don't harbor the type of fondness for you I would need to make you my wife. I beg you not to live in your dream world any longer. I cannot play along. I ask your forgiveness for any embarrassment you might feel by calling off the wedding, but it's better to suffer a little embarrassment now than to be miserable for the rest of our lives, isn't it?"

"Oh, pshaw. You'll change your mind by the time I return. Which brings me to my real reason for stopping by today. I must make a trip to Hartford for at least a month, perhaps longer. My friend from finishing school, Joan Dillard, has asked me to visit, and that means of course I must visit all my relations who live in the area or they will be quite offended. You understand."

"Of course."

"And of course I must make a special side trip to see my great-aunt Nora. She has been ill."

"I'm so sorry to hear that. I pray she will recover quickly."

"That's the first thing you've said all day that sounds like you possess the least bit of warmth," Hazel pointed out.

"Blame it on the cold weather," he quipped. "After all, my house is freezing, as you reminded me."

Hazel eyed the fireplace near Nash's desk. "Now that you mention it, it is getting colder in here. You allow the servants to be much too slothful, Nash. Really, you need me to run this household with an iron fist. We can't marry a moment too soon."

If Hazel were the type of woman he could love, Nash would have run into her arms, stroked her hair, and murmured sweet words about the long-awaited day. But he couldn't. Judging from Hazel's frigid look and stiff demeanor, she didn't miss any signs of longing or affection.

He couldn't marry Hazel. Not today, not next month, not ever.

٭

Becca stood on the street and looked at a row of fine homes. She had to keep trying. Maybe people on a different street would be friendlier than the ones she'd seen so far. No one had been helpful except for that nice maid who, for some reason unknown to her, worked for that awful woman. In other circumstances she and the maid might have been friends. Becca kept walking past the John Brown house.

POWER STREET.

"Maybe this is it. Maybe I will find God's power on this street." Her mood lightened by her silly joke, she tried a couple of other houses without success. The afternoon sun would disappear soon. She had to find something.

She watched a fashionable woman depart from the next house. She didn't turn Becca's way, so she couldn't see the woman's face, but Becca had no doubt it bore aristocratic features. The woman boarded a fine conveyance, and she was soon on her way. If she were the mistress of the house, maybe it wasn't a good time to ask about a position. Or maybe the woman was a daughter. Regardless, Becca had no time to waste speculating. She went to the back.

Even in the cold, the kitchen window had been left open a crack. Surely the fire burned hot in this house. Peering into the back-door window, Becca saw a congenial-looking woman with gray hair and plump arms pulling a cake from the hearth. Becca wished she hadn't smelled such a sweet aroma to remind her she had run out of her own house before lunch. A wiry maid with a hooked nose sat at the table, polishing silver forks with a cloth blackened by her work. She knocked, and the maid dropped a fork.

"I'm sorry," Becca called through the door. "I didn't mean to scare ya."

The maid grimaced and picked up the utensil before approaching the back door. "We weren't expecting anybody. Not just yet, anyway. Who are you?"

"I–I'm Becca Hanham. I'm here about a job."

"Already? Harrod worked fast." She saw Becca's satchel. "Set that in the corner. I'll show ya to yer room later."

Becca felt as though she'd been thrown in the middle of a story without reading the first chapters. But since the maid seemed friendly, she didn't ask questions. The cook was in the process of forming dough into a loaf. The yeasty aroma promised the baked bread would taste delectable. Becca hoped if she were hired here, her pay included meals.

"I'm glad to see ya, girlie. I got plenty o' work fer ya," the cook said.

The maid nodded. "Let me tell Harrod you're here."

Becca felt nervous. The cook eyed her with a bit too much happiness.

"But I hadn't sent word yet," she heard a man protest just outside the kitchen door.

"Well, somebody's here."

A man that Becca figured to be Harrod, with a proud carriage and well-kept white hair, entered the kitchen and studied her from head to toe. "Who are you and how did you hear about the position? I haven't sent word yet."

She filled him in on her personal details. "I—I didn't hear about a job, really, but I'm lookin'."

"We're hirin'," Cook said. "Our scullery maid eloped with the neighbor's footman this mornin', and I'm needin' help here. So do ya want the job or not?"

Harrod scowled at the cook. "I am in charge here. You are to remember that."

She shrank from him. "Yes, sir."

Becca tried not to quiver. If Harrod could make a strong woman such as Cook obey without question, he must be influential indeed.

The butler turned his attention to Becca. "She is right. We are in need of a scullery maid, and with so many women working in the factories nearby, household help is short. You will find that young Mr. Abercrombie is quite generous with his servants, and the work here is far less dangerous than many of the positions you'll find in manufacturing. We offer room and board, Thursday afternoons off, and an allowance of two dollars a week."

The offer was a far cry from the good relationship she might have with children, but without any other offers and snow falling with a vengeance just beyond the window, her choices seemed too limited for her to refuse. Besides, the idea of helping a cook appealed to her. Maybe she could learn new dishes to prepare at home. She nodded as she curtsied. "I accept."

"Good. That is a very wise decision, I assure you," Harrod said.

"Now that the master's home, we'll want everythin' to go just so," Cook said. "Even though he breaks me heart when he won't let me cook him a nice lobster." She placed both hands over her heart as though the motion would hold it together.

"Your opinions are not important," Harrod chastised her. "You are here to serve." He looked at Becca without blinking. "And that applies to you, as well, girlie. Don't forget it." Having dispensed his advice, he departed the kitchen.

Cook shook her head. "He likes to look strict, and I reckon he is. But he has a soft heart, that one."

As interesting as Harrod appeared, Becca wondered more about her new employer. "You say the master's home? Home from where?"

Cook handed her a bonnet and apron. "Home from a business trip abroad. Went all over Europe to increase business, he did. He's in charge of the tradin' company he inherited from his father now, and lots of people depend on him."

"He sounds very important." She hoped she would be worthy to work even as a scullery maid for someone so prominent.

"Oh, he is."

"Is he very old?"

Cook guffawed. "No, child. He's a bachelor still, livin' all alone here with just us servants. It's high time he married. Though I wish he warn't marryin' the one that's runnin' after him."

The master seemed more and more interesting. "Oh?"

The older woman shook her head. "I shouldn't have said that much. Now there's no more time for chat. There's work to be done." She escorted Becca to the scullery just off the kitchen and pointed to a mound of pots in need of scrubbing.

With effort she kept her mouth from dropping open upon seeing so much work waiting for her. "If there's just the master, then why so many pots?"

Cook shook her head. "You don't expect the servants to starve, do ya? We have to fix them their meals, too. And speakin' of servants, I come from a long line of servants. I'm a McIntire."

"Oh, I know some of yer clan, then. Patrick and Joseph play with me brothers."

"Yea, them's me nephews. I know who ya are." Pity filled her eyes. She clucked her tongue, and Becca realized the cook was aware of her father's reputation as a drunk.

"Seems like ever'body knows ever'body." Impoverishment was no shame. She could have held her head up, if only

Father with his drinking and slovenly ways hadn't besmirched their name.

"Now, now, girlie. What yer father does or don't do ain't yer fault. Besides, ye're startin' yer own life now." Her voice became brisk. "As soon as ye're done there, ye'll be helpin' me with the master's dinner."

"What's fer dinner?" Images of food she had never eaten but only heard about—oyster stew, tender roast pork drenched with brown gravy, vegetables swimming in a sauce of butter and cream, and the cake that had just come out of the oven—popped into her mind.

"The master asked fer clear soup, bread, and cheese. I declare, sometimes my talents are wasted here." She glanced at the cooling cake on the counter. "He'll usually take dessert if I have it, though. That's why I made it."

"Oh!" Becca couldn't help but eye the fluffy-looking treat as though she were an ant at a picnic. She inhaled to allow its sweet scent to fill her nostrils.

Cook chuckled. "There'll be enough fer ya to have a thin slice. The master don't mind. He can't eat a whole cake anyway."

"But what about the rest of dinner?" If she had enough money to live in a fine home and pay servants well, she'd eat like a queen every night. "If he's eatin' that poor, are we servants on bread and water?" Eager for information, she had blurted the term "servant" for the first time in reference to herself. The idea sounded so strange she wondered if she could ever become accustomed to it.

Cook let out a hearty laugh. "We'll be havin' the same. I know that sounds odd, and in most fine homes, I'd venture it would be odd. But he lives simply. All that'll change when Miss Caldwell becomes his wife. Mark my words. Now off to the scullery with ya. Ye've got work to do."

Scrubbing pots wasn't easy, but she already knew that

from her chores at home. Throwing herself into the task, she relished the chance to prove her worth. If she failed at this job, an unwanted match with Micah awaited.

Soon she heard Cook's exasperation. "I've got soup to prepare. Why must she leave the silver in the way?"

Becca rushed to the main part of the kitchen and saw Cook with her hands on her hips, shaking her head at silver implements on the table. "Shall I move those, Cook?"

Cook thought for a moment, then looked at the kitchen door. "No tellin' where she went. Oh, all right, girlie." She picked up a set of silver candlesticks with marble orbs in the center and matching marble platforms on the ends. "I think she's gettin' ready for Miss Caldwell to visit. She demands that all the silver stay shiny whether or not it's bein' used at the moment. She looks in the drawers, ya know." Cook scrunched her nose. "Here. Put these in the sidebar in the dinin' room."

Becca took them and found herself surprised by their substantial weight. "Yes, ma'am."

One candlestick in each hand, she pushed open the door that was already ajar and entered the formal dining room. She'd prepared herself to see luxurious furnishings, but when she saw the extent of the room, she stopped and took a breath. The space seemed more immense than her entire home. A mahogany dining table with twelve matching seats beckoned guests to a party. Carved corner cabinets displayed dishes too pretty to use for eating—even for formal dining. Oil paintings of floral arrangements added beauty to the room, as did a table runner with intricate embroidery. Brass candlesticks with tapered, cream-colored beeswax candles adorned the table.

Gawking too long wouldn't be advisable, since Cook was sure to call her back into the scullery if she lingered. She looked for the sidebar and found a heavy piece of furniture with a mirror. It had two rows of drawers she suspected held utensils and table linens. On the bottom, two doors looked as though they concealed spaces tall enough for the candlesticks to be stored standing. She decided to try one of those. As she shifted both candlesticks to one hand so she could open the door, one dropped. The *thud* it made against the floor made the chime in the floor clock across the room vibrate.

"Oh!" She gasped. Bending down to retrieve the fallen stick, she realized her hands shook, and her heart beat with such fear her body felt like one big pulse.

Cook ran into the room. "Girlie! What happened?"

"I–I'm sorry. I dropped one. I didn't mean for that to happen."

Harrod entered. "What is all the commotion?"

Cook pointed at Becca. "She dropped a candlestick. She didn't mean no harm."

"Give that to me." Harrod extended his hand and took the candlestick. Becca watched, still shaking, as he inspected it. "No harm done. Amazing." He looked at the floor. Bending toward it, he squinted and pointed. "What is that I see? A dent?" He pursed his lips.

"She didn't mean it," Cook protested.

"No, I didn't."

Harrod looked her in the eye. "You have done irreparable damage to the master's residence. Such clumsiness will not be tolerated. Miss Hanham, pack your belongings and prepare to leave at once. You are dismissed."

three

From his upstairs study, Nash heard voices in the dining room. The butler sounded upset, a condition unlike his usual composed self. Nash ventured into the room to assess the situation.

He saw Harrod, silver-and-marble candlestick in hand, along with Cook and a servant he'd never before seen. He studied the girl and was struck by how familiar she seemed. Who was she? "I say, what's happening here?"

Taken by surprise, Harrod straightened, then answered, "Mr. Abercrombie, sir. I beg your forgiveness. I was quite distracted by an incident here, and I didn't hear you come in."

Judging from her mode of dress, Nash discerned the girl was the new scullery maid. Try as he might, he couldn't keep from staring at the brunette beauty.

The girl surveyed him, fear lighting her eyes. She blushed and averted her gaze to her feet.

"The girl will be gone within a quarter hour. You have my word," Harrod said.

Nash shook his head and held up his palm. "Wait."

The girl looked back up with crystal blue eyes peeking at him from under midnight black eyelashes. Her pale, heart-shaped face stirred a memory; suddenly he knew. Before him stood the girl who sold him that box of lucifers so many years ago. Except now she was a woman. An extraordinary-looking young woman. The light in her eyes told him she recognized him, too. Her lips parted, and her fear seemed to diminish. If only he could paint a portrait to capture such loveliness!

"Where is she going?" he asked Harrod without looking at him.

"Sir?" he responded. "Why, I suppose she shall be returning to her home."

Nash kept looking at her. Just seeing her brought to his heart emotions he'd never felt, emotions far beyond compassion and pity. He was drawn to her in a way he had never been drawn to a woman. The feelings took him by surprise in their existence—and their intensity. He could hardly speak. "Whatever for?"

Harrod touched his arm. "Sir, this, this—girl, dropped one of your dearly departed mother's candlesticks and caused a dent in the dining room floor that I do not believe can ever be repaired. If you will inspect the damage, sir." He pointed to a small nick in the floor, causing Nash finally to take his gaze from the new maid.

"Oh, that. Well." He searched for a defense. "That could have been made by my boot this very morning. And as for those candlesticks, I never liked them."

"But, sir!" Harrod protested.

Nash focused on the girl. "What is your name, miss?"

She curtsied. "Becca. Becca Hanham, sir."

Seeing her legs shake in fear, he felt pity.

"I–I'm sorry for my mistake, sir. I pray you will forgive me."

"That's all I needed to hear. Becca, you shall remain in my employ if that should please you."

She blushed a most flattering shade of rose. "I couldn't ask for a better answer to my prayers, sir."

"You were actually praying that I could keep you on as my scullery maid?" Nash couldn't imagine anyone wanting a job of low station so much.

She looked him in the eye. "Yes, sir. I've seen the Lord answer prayer before, and He sure did this time."

"Indeed." Nash smiled at her, and her face softened.

Harrod cleared his throat. "Of course your decision is final, Mr. Abercrombie. She will continue to function as your scullery maid. However, I assure you, never will she touch a piece of valuable silver again." He eyed the tiny nick. "If I may say so, Miss Caldwell will be very upset to spy such a spot in a dining room where she will be entertaining once she is your wife."

Nash tried not to shudder. Though Hazel would never entertain in his home, he wanted to avoid unpleasantness with her all the same. "Please have it filled in, then, if possible."

"I'll do my best. Restoring it now would certainly be wise."

"She's going on a trip to Hartford. There should be time to have it repaired before she returns."

"Yes, sir." Harrod examined the nick once more. "The cost could be considerable. May I suggest we subtract the amount from the girl's pay to compensate for the damage? She should not have been so careless with that candlestick."

Harrod had his full attention. "No, I shall cover the expense. She admitted her mistake, and that is enough for me."

"Very well. You are too kind."

"Yes, sir," the girl agreed. "Thank you, sir."

Seeing her straight on, he knew for certain the match girl stood before him. He remembered the encounter well. He wasn't supposed to be out that night except he had forgotten his father's birthday—a lapse that still made him cringe to remember—and he needed to purchase a last-minute gift. He hadn't planned to stumble upon a destitute girl begging any passerby to purchase her wares. Papa's prosperity and the Abercrombie position had shielded him from the realities of child labor and deep poverty. When the Abercrombies bestowed Christian charity—and those occasions happened often—Papa made the decision. Before that evening, no one beseeched Nash for help. The girl's pitiful clothing and the way she shivered against the cold had brought him to such sorrow he felt led to buy enough lucifers to last a year and then pay more than they were worth. His generosity was his first step as a Christian man, young though he was.

Because it was the first time he'd acted on his own to give charity to another person, remembrance of the brief event stayed with him. From time to time he recalled her cherubic face and wondered what had happened to her. The unmistakable wide blue eyes, soft pink cheeks, and dark hair falling in curls spoke of her as a young woman. What a beauty she had become!

He couldn't believe it. So the girl had grown up and become his scullery maid. His heart lurched, almost stopping with happiness at finding her once more. His stomach quivered with an unfamiliar, disconcerting, and strange type of excitement. He wanted to experience it again.

Without notice or beckoning, an idea popped into his mind. An idea that could change his life forever.

ﾞﾞ

Of all the houses in Providence, she had somehow stumbled on Nash Abercrombie's—the boy she had been praying for all these years. How did that happen? Was it the Lord's doing?

The master's authoritative voice resonated in the room, and Becca recognized its beauty. The tone sounded as comforting as it had the night she first met him, but the pitch had grown deeper, more mature. Hearing him made her skin prickle in delight, much like listening to a sentimental song.

And to look at him! His very presence affected her. She hadn't expected to see him again, looking so comely with lustrous hair that rippled like the bay waters at midnight and eyes as brown as a luxurious cup of coffee. His glance left her weak to the core. Becca felt her face warm. Her breathing became rapid, and her knees felt as though they could no longer hold her weight.

"Off with you, now," Harrod said, though not in too harsh a tone.

Cook nodded and gave Becca a gentle shove to prod her into the kitchen. Becca wanted to look back at the master one last time, but she knew better.

The kitchen, with its cooking aromas and warm fire, seemed like a place of sanctuary. As soon as the door shut behind them, Becca headed toward the table, pulled out a chair, and plopped into it. She couldn't resist allowing her gaze to fall toward the door. "So that was the master," she whispered.

"'Tis he." Cook made her way to Becca and placed her hand on her new charge's shoulder. "Ya had quite a scare, almost bein' fired. Good thing Mr. Abercrombie showed up when he did."

She nodded.

"Ya seem flushed." Cook touched Becca's cheek with the back of her hand. "What's the matter? Are ya ill?"

"N–no." She may have seemed ill but felt far from it. If her feelings were illness, she wished she could be sick all the time. To demonstrate Cook need not worry that Becca couldn't work, she forced herself to stand.

"But I wouldn't imagine ye'd be expectin' to see the master yet. And ya won't be seein' him any more tonight, either." Cook shooed her new scullery maid with a swoop of her hand. "He'll be with us tomorrow mornin' at prayer time. But ye're to speak to him only if ye're spoken to, ya hear?"

"Oh." He would never remember her. She felt her hopes that she could ever thank him melt.

"Ya do understand." Cook's voice sounded sterner than Becca had heard from her. "Harrod hired ya to do yer work invisible-like. Ya ain't allowed to take liberties in talkin' to anybody who'd employ ya, or you'll be turned out on yer ear in no time."

So she was no longer a person. "I understand."

"I have a feelin' ya ain't used to bein' a scullery maid, are ya?"

She shook her head.

"Haven't ya ever worked a day in yer life?"

"Of course. At home."

Cook waved her hand at Becca. "No wonder ye're so sheltered. Ye're a pretty girlie. I imagine ye'll be movin' on to better things shortly. But for now, do yer best at the job before ya, and all will work out. Especially if ya take my advice and behave as ye're expected. Ya see, us downstairs servants ain't allowed to be visible to the master. If he sees ya, look down at the floor and stay still till he passes."

This advice came as a shock. "That don't seem polite. Not so much as a greetin'?"

"Never. Speakin' to the master's very impolite. And you most assuredly don't want ta speak to his new wife once he marries." While Becca hid her thoughts, Cook rattled on. "Just between you and me and the fence post, I don't much like that woman what's been chasin' him. But I'm just a cook, so I got no say in the matter." Cook leaned close enough to whisper. "Her name's Hazel. We servants call her Witch Hazel." She laughed so that her chest bobbed up and down, but she clapped her hand over her lips to stifle herself.

How horrible this Hazel woman must be. Yet no matter how awful she was, no one in Becca's station stood a chance with an Abercrombie. Discouraged, she retreated to the scullery and busied herself with the pots. She scrubbed through the dinner hour, wondering when she would be able to eat her portion of delicious-smelling soup, but it stood to reason that the servants would eat after the master and then the upstairs servants.

"Cook?"

The older woman stopped kneading dough long enough to answer. "Yea?"

"Do you think I could go home long enough to tell my parents where I am? I'm afraid Mother might worry."

Cook glanced outside and nodded toward the black night and newly fallen snow. "She'd worry more if she knew ya was walkin' the streets this late. No, ye'd best go to bed. Ya can have a bit o' leisure before ya shut yer eyes. Six thirty comes mighty early in the mornin'."

"Six thirty?"

"If I was you, I'd rise at six. Ye're lucky ya don't work for a large household with lots of servants. If ya did, the pile of dishes ye'd be lookin' at t'would be three times as high." She glanced around the kitchen and grinned. "Ah, this is an easy life."

Becca doubted "easy" was the word, but gratitude for any mercy the Lord showed filled her heart. Thursday would arrive in a day. Then she'd go home and tell her parents what transpired.

Harrod entered.

"Yer cocoa's up soon." Cook's voice betrayed her impatience.

"I am not here for that." Harrod regarded Becca. "Girlie, Mr. Abercrombie wishes to speak with you."

Using her peripheral vision, Becca could see Cook's eyes widen. Becca pointed to herself. "Me? Have I done somethin' else wrong already?"

"He says not. I do not know what his business is with you. Come with me."

Becca looked down at her clothing, splattered with grease, water, and soap. "May I freshen meself?"

"There is no time. He awaits."

Though Harrod lingered at the kitchen door, Becca had to speak to Cook. "Ya—ya didn't say I did a poor job, did ya?"

"Oh no. Ya did a fine job, especially for one not used to such work. Why, I'd tell the master meself, if I wasn't so busy."

Becca nodded. She believed Cook hadn't complained about

her. She had no reason since Becca had been careful to be obedient and industrious. She wasn't as sure Cook wanted to face the master to defend Becca.

"Come along, girlie," Harrod prodded. "You won't find out what Mr. Abercrombie wants as long as you keep standing here."

Trying to hide shaking hands by keeping them clasped, Becca followed Harrod through the house. While the furnishings and decor told the story of a wealthy man, the setting didn't strike her to be as ostentatious as the house where she was interviewed by the aloof woman. She hoped her meeting with the master would go better than that.

When they arrived at the study on the third floor, Harrod announced her. She entered, and Harrod shut the door behind her. Nash sat in a leather chair behind his desk. She held back a gasp with wonder at being so close to him once again. Nash's face looked even more handsome and kind than she remembered. To be working for a man who exuded such generosity of spirit was nothing less than a gift from God. Yet she could only be a servant to him. And if she'd done something wrong to cause her dismissal, she'd lose even that status.

Avoiding his gaze so as not to appear bold, she observed her surroundings. To her surprise, his study was small and dark with nautical touches. The room contrasted to Mrs. Gill's spacious and light sitting room enhanced by floral wallpaper. Two hurricane lamps on Mr. Abercrombie's desk provided him light. She withheld a smile. Perhaps a man felt more at ease in an atmosphere akin to a ship's cabin rather than a rose-colored loft flooded with sun. She also noticed a fixed ladder left of the doorway and a hatch above. This must have been the access to the widow's walk on his home. A small fire glowed in the hearth. However, his presence made the room seem as warm as the most appealing early summer day. Still, she approached him with trepidation, not looking him in the face. She felt uncomfortable talking to the master alone in defiance of her earlier instructions to do everything possible to stay invisible to him. She hoped she wouldn't make a fool of herself. She said a prayer for wisdom.

He stood to greet her, revealing a fine figure of a young man. The gesture gave her the impression that he could treat her as a person of high station—an experience unknown to her. "Sit down, please." He motioned to the chair in front of his desk. The fact he offered her a seat surprised her.

He returned to the leather chair behind his desk. She noticed it held papers stacked in neat piles that weren't too large. No doubt he paid every paper bill on time, maybe even before it was due. "No doubt you already know that I am Nash Abercrombie."

"Y–yes, sir." She stole a glance of his face and held her breath.

"Do you know why I summoned you?"

She clasped her hands more tightly. "No, sir. I hope my work is satisfactory. If it ain't, I can learn. I promise. My mother says I always catch on real good." Realizing she rambled and had repeated an unfortunate phrase that brought her unspoken insult before, she bit her lip.

He smiled with warmth. "I have no doubt you are smart. Very smart. And as for your work, I've heard no complaints. I have another reason for summoning you. I wanted to see if you are who I think you are. Did you perchance ever sell lucifers on Meeting Street?"

"I did." So maybe that's what this was all about. "So ya remember the night ya saved my life." Her voice sounded more hopeful than she meant, and her smile felt too wide.

"Yes, I do recall that bitter night. But you say I saved your life? I hardly think I can credit myself with such a noble deed."

"Oh, but ya did! If ya hadn't come along when ya did, I'd of stayed out in that cold, dark night till I froze to death. Cook told me I'm supposed to be invisible and not talk to ya none, so I hope ya don't mind if I take this chance to tell ya thank ya, sir. Ya have my eternal gratitude, and I promise to work hard while I'm in yer employ to show just how grateful I am."

"You need not work harder than you must. An honest day's work is all I expect from anyone in my employ." He leaned forward. "I admit, I was drawn to you when I saw you here, just as I was drawn to you when you were selling lucifers all those years ago. I never could explain why something in your eyes caught my attention, but I never forgot you."

Though his eyes held nothing but kindness, a fleeting thought unsettled her. She'd heard stories of unscrupulous masters, and she wasn't about to relinquish her virtue to him or any man. Perhaps she shouldn't have mentioned just how grateful she was. "Thank ya, sir." She looked at her cotton-covered knees.

To her relief, she heard him shift back in his chair, so she summoned the courage to return her gaze to him.

"I was only out that night to run an important errand. It was not my habit to wander the streets in the dark, but I'm glad I had the chance to buy lucifers from you." He paused. "Tell me about yourself."

She flinched. What could she tell him? That her family lived in poverty? That her father insisted she wed an oaf or get a job because of yet another new baby on the way? After taking a deep breath, she told him about her life. The version she recounted softened the harsh reality without engaging in a fib.

His eyes showed compassion. "I don't find your situation surprising. I understand you had no chance to return home since you were just hired. Does your mother know where you are?"

"No, sir."

He glanced at a small clock on his desk. "It's far too late for you to wander the streets alone. I'll have a messenger send word to your family."

"Thank ya, sir." She thought for a moment and asked, "Are ya always so kind to yer servants?"

"I hope they all think me kind, although I have set my attention on you in particular for a reason. I have a question for you. You have nothing to lose by answering, even if your response is to decline." He let out a breath, as if bolstering himself to ask.

What could make him nervous, such a powerful man asking a favor of a mere scullery maid?

"Go ahead," she prodded, hoping he didn't mind.

"My request is unorthodox. . ."

There was that word again. Apparently it was quite popular with the upper classes. She resolved to find out what it meant.

". . .and I pray you won't be offended, but you see, I'm in quite a pinch and I really need your help."

"My help? But I ain't nothin' but a maid, and the lowest maid at that. What could I possibly do for ya?"

"Something I hope you will find easy." He took in another breath. "Miss Hanham, will you marry me?"

four

Becca felt too astounded to answer. From a scullery maid to a fiancée in a matter of hours? No, he couldn't be proposing marriage.

"I can see from the expression on your face that you're shocked. Of course you are," he said matter-of-factly. "I didn't ask you in the proper manner." To Becca's further surprise, he rose and made his way toward her. "Would you stand, please?"

Too amazed to do anything but obey, she did.

He bent down on one knee and took her hands in his. "Becca Hanham, will you marry me?"

She wished she could sit in a chair nearby, for the feeling of weakness in her knees once again made its presence known. Instead she summoned her strength and answered, "Sir, this must be a joke."

His face turned serious. "I assure you, it is not."

"You want me to marry you?" She felt dizzy with emotion.

"Yes. I know you weren't expecting me to propose, but since I noticed you, I have given the prospect thought and prayer. Please, think and pray on it overnight if you like." Still he remained on his knee.

"I don't need that much time. I–I'm flattered. More than flattered." Never would she have imagined a man of such importance bending his knee before her. A vision of Micah entered her head. His future wife would be lucky if he demanded marriage before belching and then insisting that she pour him a portion of ale. Becca wished her position in society would permit her to wed the man before her. "Please, you don't have to stay on yer knee."

With the agility of a sportsman, he arose. The thought occurred to Becca that other than seeing his house and learning about his servants, she knew almost nothing about this man. But that wasn't the only reason she hesitated. "I can't accept. I don't know why ya took leave of yer senses, but once ya wake up, ye'll see yer family wouldn't allow us to wed."

Deep sadness filled his countenance, and she wished she hadn't caused it. "I was the only child of my parents, may the Lord rest their souls, and I have no other family. At least, not any family close enough in relationship with me to care or to be affected in any significant way by our marriage."

Thinking of her large family, the idea of such solitude made her sad. Yet Nash didn't live outside of the world like a monk. He knew people. "But yer friends..."

"Any friends of mine who wouldn't accept my choice of a wife are not my friends."

She felt too touched for words, but she had to respond. If he spoke the truth—and his conviction made him seem as though he did—she still worried about the consequences of the match. "Why me? And why now? I ain't nothin' but a match girl ya remember from years ago, and ye're a young man that bought me wares so I could take refuge from the bitter night. But as much as I am grateful to ya—and I am, I can promise ya that—that ain't no reason to marry me or fer me to marry ya, either."

"Do I not have enough to offer you?"

She gasped. "How could ya ask such a thing? Ya have so much to offer any woman. I know ye're a Christian. I see a Bible on your desk, and Cook told me ya lead the servants in prayers each mornin'. I want a Christian man."

"That doesn't surprise me. Your spirit is so sweet."

She felt herself blush, and she looked downward. "But I

want even more than that. Mebbe I'm expectin' too much, but I want to love—really love—the man I marry one day."

His expression softened. "Your response shows me how right I was to ask."

"Come again?"

"You obviously have no idea how many women would jump at the chance to seize me for my fortune regardless of their personal feelings for me one way or another. I realize you might not know exactly who I am, but anyone can see from my home that God has rained financial blessings on my family. And your first thought? That my marriage to you would adversely affect me. And that you don't love me. At least not yet." Becca would have sworn she almost saw mist in his eyes. "To be with someone so unaffected is refreshing. You have no idea."

She couldn't imagine any woman wanting such a compassionate and handsome man only for his fortune, but thought saying so would be much too bold. "Love is very important to me. Some might say too important. But I don't agree with 'em."

"And neither do I."

Preparing herself to say one of the hardest things she imagined she'd ever have to say in her life, Becca inhaled and steeled herself. "Then ya understand why I gotta say no."

"Please don't answer me yet. I know my question comes as a surprise. A shock, even." He glanced at the empty chair. "Please. Take a seat and hear me out."

She nodded and obeyed.

He returned to his seat behind his desk, crossing his arms as he settled into position. "I know it sounds harsh, but I have a reason for my proposal. You see, I wish to discourage a woman named Hazel Caldwell. She's a member of my set and has many family connections, but I have every reason to believe that her family fortune is dwindling and she's looking for security. She sees my money as her security."

"How awful!" Becca blurted before she could stop herself. Embarrassed, she looked at her lap. "I'm sorry. I should never have said that."

Nash's mouth twisted into a rueful curve. "Truth be told, I can hardly expect any woman not to consider my fortune when thinking of marriage to me. But I want my future wife to consider me as a person, just as I would consider her—as I consider you—a person. You and I are alike, you see. I don't believe it's right for me to marry a woman I don't love and who doesn't love me."

So Cook had been right! Mr. Abercrombie was in a terrible romantic mess with a frightful woman.

Nash continued. "I realize we don't know each other well enough to discern love or not. We need not wed right away. Could we use our engagement as a time to get to know one another? I vow to you that if you decide not to go through with the wedding, I will set you free with no further obligation whatsoever."

Thinking through his offer, Becca didn't answer right away.

"Perhaps I do sound foolish." He leaned toward her, and his eyes looked imploring. "Do you think me ridiculous to want to marry for love?"

"No, sir."

His smile was bittersweet. "You are so lucky, Miss Hanham. You don't have to consider society and position when you wed. You are free to marry whomever you like."

"That ain't so, sir."

He startled. "Oh?"

"Ya see, I'm only here 'cause me father said I had to find a job or marry somebody I don't love."

"Really?" Surprise registered on his expression, and his eyes held a questioning look.

Becca could only imagine that he wondered, without

fortunes and connections to consider, why there would be a need for her father to suggest a loveless match. Sheltered from poverty as Nash was, Becca doubted he could comprehend deep desire to improve one's lot in whatever way, however miniscule. She might explain that to him. One day, but not now.

"You left the marriage out of the story you told me before," he pointed out, choosing discretion.

"I didn't think ye'd care about it, to tell the truth."

He smiled. "I suppose if I were an ordinary employer, I wouldn't. But I'm glad you told me. The fact that you might be able to understand my predicament gives me some consolation."

"Yes, I do." If only Becca could agree to his solution, but she was still unsure. "There must be a lot of grand ladies who'd want to marry ya, Mr. Abercrombie, if ya don't mind me sayin' so. What about one o' them?"

"They consider me unavailable because Miss Caldwell is a force with whom to be reckoned." He shrugged. "I may have the power to change the right woman's mind, but I don't feel drawn to them enough to pursue anything beyond an acquaintanceship."

Becca felt pity for the master, a surprising emotion considering that by all appearances, he sat on top of the world. His servants knew him as a captain of commerce in Providence. "I—I don't know what to say."

"Don't say anything. Let me summon my driver, Jack, to take you home tonight. I don't think he's gone to the pub yet. Take the morning off, and give me your answer during afternoon tea tomorrow.

❧

Later, Nash escorted Becca to his carriage and helped her embark. With amusement and pleasure, he noted how she observed the conveyance with wide eyes, much as she had noticed the house. So in awe was she that she seemed to be walking in glass slippers, reminding him of the little cinder girl in the old fairy tale. He hoped he could be Becca's prince.

Returning to his study to tidy up the last bit of remaining correspondence, Nash found himself daydreaming about Becca. When he told her he had prayed about whether or not to ask her hand in marriage, he had not exaggerated. The open Bible he had left on the table beside his chair told a tale of how he had consulted scripture as he prayed. The fact Becca was not the expected choice for him would indeed cause consternation in certain quarters, but his heart told him the fair young lady was worth getting to know. Being with her as a potential wife would never be possible if she were to remain his servant, but his daring proposal put her in a new position. If Becca agreed to give him a chance, he felt certain the feelings she had already stirred in his heart would grow. If only time spent together would cause love to pour into her heart as well. He hoped he could make her life a better one, not with riches but with a lifetime of love.

Lord, Thy will be done in this matter.

ð

Mother was in her room tending to the babies, Father was out, and her other brothers and sisters occupied themselves with their own concerns and were not impressed by her comings and goings, so Becca managed to sneak through the front room without being noticed. A lingering scent of porridge didn't tempt her, even though she never had partaken of soup at the Abercrombie house. Excitement had overcome hunger.

She headed for the room in back she shared with many sisters. She hoped to find clean water in the plain white pitcher to wash her face so she wouldn't have to fetch it herself. Eyeing the small oak vanity, she didn't assess the rest of the room as she walked toward the corner.

"What are ya doin' here?" Naomi's voice pierced the air.

Becca jumped and clutched her hand to her chest. "Ya scared me to death!"

"I'm sorry," a nightshift-clad Naomi apologized, hairbrush in hand. "Ya scared me to death, too!" Recovering in a flash, Naomi looked into a small mirror that had been her Christmas gift. She studied herself before nodding and placing the hairbrush they all shared on the vanity beside the pitcher. "So did ya get a job?"

"Yea, in a fine home for a wonderful master. He lives all alone except for his servants. A devoted lot, they are, but no family." She sighed. "Much has changed since this morning."

"Oh?"

Becca hesitated, wondering if she should take her sister into her confidence. But she and Naomi had always been close in age and spirit, and the urge to tell someone hounded her. She decided to trust her sister. "The young master asked me to marry him."

Naomi plopped onto the nearest mattress. "What? He asked you to marry him? The master of a fine house? I don't believe it."

"I can hardly believe it myself."

"Ya think he meant it?"

"I—I do."

Naomi gasped. "Oh, Becca! What are ya goin' to do?"

Becca placed her forefinger on puckered lips. "Shh! Not so loud. I ain't said nothin' to nobody but you."

"And it's a good thing, too. We don't know nothin' about livin' like society people." She beamed. "But you'll find out soon."

Becca sat by Naomi. "I ain't accepted yet. And I ain't sure I'm gonna."

"Why not?" Naomi clasped her hands to her chest and looked upward. Becca could see from the faraway look on her face that she saw not the cracked ceiling, but a vision from a different world in another part of Providence. "Just think. Ye'll never have to work again. Ya can wear dresses that make ya look like ya came out of a store window. Ya can eat rich food and sleep till noon. Mebbe I can visit and we can have tea on a fancy silver service and those little sandwiches that my friend May says she has to fix for her mistress." She gasped and clutched Becca's knee. "You'll be the first person we know who'll be the mistress of a manor instead of just a servant girl." As her excitement increased, her voice grew louder.

"Shh! I told ya I ain't sure I'm gonna accept. The more ya talk, the more I think mebbe I shouldn't. He don't know nothin' about our family, how we live." Becca couldn't help but compare her current surroundings to the Abercrombie residence. What would Nash think once he set foot in such a place?

Naomi eyed their room and sighed. When she spoke, her discouraged tone of voice told of her agreement. "When do ya have to tell him one way or the other?"

"I promised I'd show up for afternoon tea tomorrow." The thought made her nervous. She had little idea what to do at a formal tea, even alone with the man who would be her fiancé. "I might not consider it at all," she said, omitting how his mere presence made her feel light as a butterfly living in fairyland, "but I'm grateful to him fer savin' my life that night—the night I told ya about."

Naomi didn't have to think long. Becca had told the story often. "Ya mean that's the same young man what paid ya so much fer that box of lucifers?"

Becca nodded.

"That's gotta be the Lord's doin'. Why else would ya land in his house of all places?"

The notion had occurred to Becca. "I know it. Especially

after I knocked on so many doors before that." She sighed. "And now I feel sorry fer him. He's got this awful woman chasin' him."

"How do ya know she's awful? Have ya met her?"

"No. But he don't paint a flatterin' picture of her. Her name is Hazel, and the servants call her Witch Hazel behind her back."

Naomi giggled. She tilted her nose upward and took on an affected accent. "I suppose she talks very snooty."

Becca grinned in spite of herself but then turned serious. "I ain't never met her, but I don't imagine I'll sound too educated against someone like her."

"True." Naomi looked worried. "I don't mean to hurt yer feelin's, but ya ain't no fine lady, and anybody breathin' can tell soon as ya open yer mouth."

"Only me own sister could get away with an insult like that." Becca scrunched her nose and rubbed her knuckles on Naomi's back in a playful manner, a gesture the sisters had always shared.

"Ya know I speak the truth." Naomi slapped at Becca's knee with a strike that didn't sting. "And I worry. You ain't got no decent dresses, neither. He's gonna be expectin' ya to be a hostess sooner or later. How are ya plannin' to fit in with all those society women?"

Having concentrated on Nash, Becca hadn't thought about his friends. Anxiety gripped her midsection. "I don't know. Mebbe I'm not supposed to fit in but be meself."

"Ye'll be laughed out o' Providence."

"Mebbe not. The Lord can perform miracles." A feeling of nervousness struck, and Becca felt she needed consolation and comfort. "How's about we ask now?" Becca took her sister's hands, and they prayed.

Father entered. "What you two girls prayin' about?" As usual, he hadn't bothered to knock.

"Nothin'." Naomi dropped her sister's hands, crossed her arms, and narrowed her eyes at her father.

"Becca will tell me. Won't ya, girl?" His voice took on a tone that told her she'd feel the sting of his belt on her legs if she didn't.

She swallowed. "I got a job."

"What is it? A nanny like ya planned?"

"No, sir. A maid."

"Oh." His voice deflated. "How much they payin' you?"

Temptation to tell him a dollar fifty knocked on her brain, but she shook it aside. "Two dollars a week plus room and board."

"Humph." He wagged his finger at her. "You be sure to bring me that money every week."

A realization occurred to Becca. "I might not be able to."

"And why not?" His voice held a challenge.

Naomi shook her head, warning her not to reveal everything yet. But considering Father's determination to squeeze her salary from her, telling all seemed to be the only option. "I might not be a maid long. I—I might not even be a maid now. The master—Nash Abercrombie—said he wants to marry me."

Father's laughter filled the room so much the thin walls seemed to shake. "You? You, girl? What are they feedin' ya up on top of that hill? Whiskey? If they are, must be mighty good. Bring me some next time ya come home, eh?"

Becca's face warmed in humiliation, but she couldn't deny the story sounded preposterous. "I'm doin' him a favor, he says. He wants to get rid of a fortune seeker."

Father's mouth slackened before he let out a boisterous chortle. "Does he now? Is he outta his head? Ye're nothin' but a Hanham. What makes him think ya don't want his fortune, too?"

Becca thought for a moment. How did he know, indeed?

Perhaps because she never dreamed of any fortune and he realized that. Besides, he asked her to marry him when such a proposal never entered her mind. She remembered his references to her spirit. "He knows I'm a woman of faith."

"That may be, but I'll wager he'll drop ya like a hot potato as soon as he gets rid of this fortune seeker he's talkin' about." He nodded, rubbing his chin. "At least ya can take advantage of the situation. Collect as many trinkets as ya can before he gets tired o' ya. Tell him ya want big diamonds and rubies."

Diamonds and rubies? The thought hadn't entered her head. She never ventured where people expected women to wear fine jewels. On the contrary, in her part of town sparkling stones would only attract thieves and thugs.

Disgust filled her being. Leave it to Father to suggest she collect as many diamonds and rubies as possible to secure her future—and his supply of ale. Still, his admonitions made her feel uneasy. Father was a man of the world and knew the ways of men. What if his warnings were true? What if Nash Abercrombie left her high and dry as soon as Hazel Caldwell was out of sight? The idea of trinkets didn't comfort her, but made her feel like a woman for hire. "I don't think I'll accept his proposal."

"That might be a good idea," Naomi said.

"Mind yer own business, Naomi." Scowling, Father crossed his arms and planted his feet on the floor. "I've heard of that Abercrombie family. They got plenty o' money. Ya better accept that offer if ya know what's good fer ya."

Becca didn't have to ask what that meant. If she didn't obey, Father was sure to throw her out of the house for good. And though the noisy, crowded rooms weren't much, her home did offer shelter and the love of her mother and siblings. God commanded her to honor her parents, so she had to do as her father insisted. Too bad the Bible never promised all parents would look out for the best interests of their children above their own.

She prayed for the courage to face whatever her future held.

five

The following day Nash returned home early from the office for afternoon tea. Not that he had accomplished much at work anyway. All he could think about was his proposal of marriage and what answer Becca might give him.

Sitting fitfully in the chair in his study, he tried to read the paper, but a story on another bank robbery didn't hold his interest. His thoughts wandered to matters of immediate concern.

Nash never envisioned that God would send the match girl from all those years before who had touched his heart. Perhaps he'd be a laughingstock for pursuing a poverty-stricken woman of low station. But simple clothing couldn't hide a sweet spirit. To Nash, that was much more valuable than an important family name. A verse from the twenty-seventh chapter of Proverbs popped into his head. "A continual dropping in a very rainy day and a contentious woman are alike." Of course the author didn't speak of Hazel, but the verse described her. He smiled in spite of himself.

Ah, Becca. Such a contrast. He prayed she would trust him enough to move forward with his proposal. If she did, he was determined she would never be sorry.

Harrod entered. "I am confirming that you still desire high tea for two to be served at five in the front parlor, sir."

"Yes."

"Thank you, sir." He cleared his throat but didn't look Nash in the face. "I am reluctant to mention this, but the new scullery maid did not report for work this morning. Under ordinary conditions, I would not make mention of this, but in light of her clumsiness yesterday, I felt I must. Perhaps she is embarrassed by your generosity of spirit and didn't feel worthy to continue working here. I can only speculate."

Since he'd never thought of Becca as a scullery maid, Nash had forgotten to let Harrod know about the previous night's events. "I'm so sorry, Harrod. I should have told you." He paused and studied his butler. Harrod stood erect with an expression of anticipation before Nash. "I have asked someone to marry me."

Harrod didn't smile. "Have you confirmed your engagement to Miss Caldwell?"

"No. I have proposed marriage to someone else."

"Indeed?" Harrod's voice rose with happiness. "If I may be so bold, do tell me about this lucky woman. I assume you met her during your trip abroad. Was it a shipboard romance, perhaps?" His eyes took on a worried light. "Those can be tricky, but if she's from a prestigious family, you may have been right to throw caution to the wind."

"Oh, I threw caution to the wind. But not aboard ship."

Harrod let a breath escape. "I must say, I am relieved you did not lose your head while crossing the Atlantic. Miss Caldwell is digging for gold, but at least we know she comes from a good family. I have heard too many stories about the riffraff who travel on ships and trains to pose as perfectly respectable people in hopes of catching a prize such as yourself. A man in your position cannot be too cautious."

"Your words are wise, and so I'm sure you'll be disappointed by my choice." He paused. "You see, there is a reason why Becca Hanham did not report for work today. Instead she is my guest for afternoon tea."

"Oh." The unflappable Harrod seemed disconcerted. "I see. Then I must make haste to find another scullery maid."

"Not yet. She has a question to answer for me first." He paused. "You see, I asked Becca Hanham to marry me."

Harrod couldn't have looked any more shocked if a tempest had struck without warning and scuttled him. "But, she is a—a scullery maid."

"Yes, I realize it's shocking. I'm a bit shocked myself. But I don't regret asking her." His voice grew stronger with determination.

"Sir, I am loath to discourage you, but. . ." He let out a slight cough. "Would you feel at ease with her in the company of your friends? Or would she?"

"I've thought of that. Certainly I don't want to subject her to ridicule. That's why, if she does accept my proposal, I'll work with her to be sure she looks and acts highborn before I open my home for a dinner party."

"If I may say so, you have much work ahead of you."

"You mean to say *we* have much work ahead of *us*. I expect you to help, you know."

Harrod sighed in the manner of an adult indulging a child. "Why did I sense you might say that? But for you, I shall comply. Anything to rid us of the prospect of Miss Caldwell."

"How many of the other servants know we hired Miss Hanham as a scullery maid?"

Harrod thought for a moment. "Other than myself, Cook and the downstairs maid. I don't believe she had time to meet anyone else."

"Good. I need all the servants to support me and not make issue of Miss Hanham's humble origins. While I will never deny her background if asked, there is no need to subject her to more gossip than necessary."

"I don't believe you'll be able to shield her forever. People will find out one way or another."

"I don't doubt it. But once they grow to love Miss Hanham for her sweet spirit, her station won't matter."

Harrod's mouth twisted, a sure sign he didn't agree. Nash

ignored the gesture. He only wanted to think of how good he could make life for Becca.

❧

Becca entered the Abercrombie residence through the back door. The appetizing scent of baking bread greeted her.

Cook spied her and stopped whisking a small green bowl containing raw eggs. "I see ya finally decided to show up fer work. Harrod told me the master knows all about it and you had the mornin' off."

"Yes, ma'am." Becca regarded dirty pots and pans that awaited washing.

"Ye're lookin' pretty today." She sniffed the air, her nostrils flailing in and out. "And I do believe I smell perfume." She eyed her charge. "Ye're lookin' and smellin' much too fancy fer a scullery maid."

Becca had dressed her best—meaning in the same dress she wore yesterday. Mother had allowed her to borrow a few precious drops of lavender-scented toilette water that Becca and her siblings saved up to buy for her as a Christmas gift just a month ago. Mother had also arranged Becca's dark hair in a flattering uplifted fashion with ringlets framing both sides of her cheeks. Before she left, Mother kissed her good-bye and gave her a tight hug. Despite the mountains of work brought about by so many siblings, Becca would miss being with her family every day.

For the first time since her birthday the previous autumn, she felt lovely. Lovely enough to face Nash and give him her answer.

Cook persisted. "Why'd ya fix yer hair up like that?"

"Mother styled it," she responded, stalling for time. Cook stared at her, so she could see there was no way out of offering a direct response. "I—I don't reckon you'd know. Mr. Abercrombie proposed marriage to me, and I'm here to give him an answer."

She dropped her fork in the bowl. "Marriage! No!" A hearty laugh filled the kitchen. "I didn't take ya for a lazy daydreamer, but that's what ya are, sure enough."

Becca paused as she tried not to be offended. Perhaps to Cook's eyes she did seem lazy and a dreamer. "No, ma'am. I'm not lazy, and I'm not a daydreamer. I can't believe it, either. But it's true." Becca filled her in on the details.

"That is a surprise, girlie. I didn't think ye'd ever be the master's match." She regarded her with a discerning eye. "Ye're mighty pretty, though, and I think ye'd be even prettier once he gets ye into better clothes."

Becca tried not to cringe.

"Any plan to get rid of Witch Hazel is a good plan in my book. She'd be a misery to work fer, she would. She tries to take over whenever she comes here as it is. But ye—now ye would understand the trials of a servant 'cause ye're a hard worker from what I seen." Cook lifted both hands in surrender. "Ah, but work! Just look at what ya done to me. Just one day out and already I'm stuck without a scullery maid."

"I'm sorry." She realized she meant it.

Cook laughed once more. "Ye'd be crazy to be sorry." She resumed whisking the eggs, her face brightening. "I'll have to ask me brother's daughter. Didn't think o' her till now."

Harrod entered. "Cook, must you speak at the top of your lungs?" He spotted Becca and his demeanor changed. "Oh, Miss Hanham. What are you doing here in the kitchen?"

"I–I'm still a scullery maid until I speak with Mr. Abercrombie, ain't I?"

He looked taken aback. "I don't suppose you have been dismissed." He cut his glance to Cook.

"She told me about the proposal. Since she works in the kitchen with me, I have a right to know." She placed her hands on her hips. "Now I ain't got a scullery maid."

"We'll discuss that later. Come along, please, Miss Hanham,

and if you plan to accept Mr. Abercrombie's proposal, remember that you are not to enter through the back door, but the front." He studied her. "Not that I ever expect you to enter alone again in any event."

The front door! She thought about the first door she had knocked on and how rude the butler had been. She'd love to knock on that front door today. Just as quickly, she put away such an indulgent thought. More important matters—and a much more important man—awaited.

"Mr. Abercrombie said he will meet you in the front parlor." Harrod led her to a room warm in temperature and inviting in atmosphere. Even a cursory examination told her that even though the decor all over the house seemed grand, the finest pieces had been saved for the best room. Chairs fashioned of carved wood and a stuffed sofa draped in silk seemed so luxurious, she feared she shouldn't sit at all, though the foot-and-claw leg designs seemed substantial.

Before she chose a seat, her gaze caught a set of portraits above the sofa. The man and woman portrayed must have been Nash's parents. If so, Nash looked just like his father, with big brown eyes and a kind but manly face. His slim-figured mother was portrayed in the high style of her time, but the expression on her lovely face didn't show the least bit of arrogance or entitlement. They must have passed on their graciousness of spirit to their son so that he didn't mind taking a chance on her, a mere servant girl.

Nash's voice sounded from behind her, catching her off guard. "Do you like those portraits?"

She jumped a bit and turned toward him.

"I'm sorry. Did I startle you? Forgive me."

Seeing him again brought back feelings of high excitement. Glad for a topic other than the answer she had to give him, she pounced upon it. "Yea, they're beautiful. I got lost lookin' at 'em."

"Those are my favorite depictions of my parents." He joined her in viewing the portraits.

"You mean there's more?" The thought of spending a great sum of money to have one portrait painted was beyond her imagination, much less commissioning several.

"Yes," he responded. "There's a set in the bedchamber they shared, painted later in their lives. And in the library is yet another portrait of the three of us when I was but a tiny babe. But this set is my favorite because the likenesses capture their happiness during the time they were a courting couple." He took them in as though seeing them for the first time. "I can stare at these paintings and forget time, too. I wish you could have known my parents. I think they would have liked you very much."

The idea warmed her spirit. "Really? How come?" The question made her sound like a small child instead of the dignified woman she wanted to be. She tried not to wince at her own embarrassment.

He didn't seem to notice her discomfiture. "They wanted a Christian woman for me, and from the way you speak of your prayer life, I know you love our Savior. And you are beautiful in appearance."

Becca felt herself blush. She averted her gaze, taking sudden interest in the arrival of the promised afternoon tea. The maid set it on the low table that looked to be created for the purpose. As Becca and Nash sat in opposite chairs around the table, the maid poured rich reddish brown liquid into china cups. Becca inhaled the scent of the hot beverage, spiced as it was, with the luxury of a cinnamon stick protruding from each cup.

Nash dismissed the maid and offered Becca a small plate of finger sandwiches, the kind Naomi said her friend May had to prepare for her mistress. Dizzy in the realization that she occupied such a position, Becca took one that looked pleasing while Nash took two.

"My father especially would have loved your spirit of adventure," he noted. "Who else would knock on doors until she found the lowest form of work? And if you agree to marry me, that will be an adventure indeed."

Holding her sandwich, she tried to speak in the manner of a highborn woman. "Indeed."

"So do you have an answer for me?"

She thought they might sit and talk a bit first, but she could see by the way his leg moved up and down with nervous energy that Nash was as anxious as she. The moment she'd been awaiting had arrived. Now that it had, she felt her heart beat all the way up to her throat. Her voice didn't want to cooperate, but she willed herself to speak from the depths of her soul. "Oh. Yes. Yes, I do. I accept your proposal." She took in a breath, not believing the words as they fell from her lips. Was she really herself—Becca Hanham, impoverished servant girl—or had she stepped into someone else's life? At the moment she didn't care, as long as she could hold on to the dream. Never had she been so happy—and so scared—at once.

Nash's eyes shone like her brother Samuel's when the big kids let him in on their games. "That is the news I wanted to hear." He took her hand in his and brushed his lips just above her knuckles. "I am honored by your acceptance."

Such words left her feeling light-headed and unable to say anything gracious. Or anything at all, really. How could someone of such stature be honored by her acceptance?

If he noticed her puny state, he hid it well. "This calls for a celebration." He summoned Harrod, who appeared in an instant. "Send Jack to the Providence Arcade for lobster."

Harrod sent Nash a knowing look that Becca didn't quite understand. "Yes, sir. If I can find him."

Nash's lips tightened. "See that you do. Miss Hanham deserves a fine meal, the first she will partake as my fiancée."

Heart still beating beyond measure, but with happiness rather than anxiety, she felt her own eyes sparkle. "I don't care if we have boiled water. I'm just happy."

"As am I. But of course, I want to make sure I have your father's blessing."

She tried not to laugh. "Father's blessin'? He'd bless a frog if he'd take me outta the house. He's tired o' feedin' me. Ya know that's why I took that job as a scullery maid to start with."

The fact she had to broach the subject of her father brought his admonitions to mind, spoiling her moment. Nash claimed happiness, but did their impending wedding please him, or just the chance to rid himself of Miss Caldwell?

When she looked back into Nash's face, she saw pity. No matter what her feelings for her father, she saw no good in turning Nash against him. "Oh, Father ain't so bad. With a brood to feed, he's gotta think about what's best fer ever'body. Accordin' to age, I'm next in line to marry. And there's a new baby on the way sometime this summer."

"A happy event indeed," Nash observed. "Even though I can't pretend to understand what it must be like to live with so many brothers and sisters, I can speculate on the difficulties your father must face. Under normal circumstances, I would have approached him before even asking you to marry me. However these are not the usual circumstances. I would feel more assured if I could confirm from him that he is agreeable to my request for your hand. I hope you understand."

"Of course." She more than understood. His concern made her feel special.

Nash eyed a small black marble statue of a pyramid on an occasional table. "But let's talk about other things while we wait for dinner to be prepared. Would you be interested in learning a bit about the trinkets I have on display in this room? Each one holds meaning for me."

Becca agreed without hesitation. Time moved at a rapid

clip as he pointed out *objets d'art* and souvenirs, talking about worlds near and far, all unknown to Becca. At first she felt nervous, realizing she had no idea about the exotic places he described. She relaxed after she could see that Nash enjoyed sharing his interests with her, even though she often felt some of her questions would sound silly to sophisticated ears. She appreciated his patience and reveled in his joy as they talked.

As the room grew dark from twilight's falling, the maid, without interrupting them, lit candles so they could see. Becca wished time would never move forward, but soon they were called to dinner. Panic and anticipation visited her when she realized that for the first time she'd be taking her meal in a real dining room, not an overcrowded area at home with too many people and too few chairs.

When they entered, they found a long table set with fine linens and dinnerware. She had never dined on a surface covered with cloth of any description. With so many people in her house, the most practical solution was for her sister to wipe bare wood with a wet rag after each meal. She doubted Father would have let Mother indulge in the purchase of linens even if they'd had the money. And cloth napkins! The men in her house, regardless of the fact the older ones knew better, were fond of wiping their mouths on their shirtsleeves. The women tried not to smear their faces so they wouldn't need napkins.

The silver looked heavy and patterned with so many flowers that Becca imagined each utensil held enough to populate a garden. Crystal glasses appeared delicate. She hoped she wouldn't break hers before the night ended. She reached for a carved chair, but Nash took it by the other side and pulled it out, nodding for her to take a seat. No man had ever pulled a seat out for her. The attention felt exciting but strange.

Nash said a blessing over the meal, a pleasant start that made her feel more comfortable with him. His words sounded so natural she could discern he wasn't putting on a show for her, a fact that relieved her. Then, following his example, she set her napkin in her lap and realized her dress was nowhere near fine enough. She needed clothing—and fast. But how could she think of a new wardrobe for herself when her family couldn't even pay for enough food? She prayed her sparse wardrobe wouldn't cause Nash embarrassment.

The hook-nosed maid Becca once thought of befriending had become her servant, presenting her with a bowl of soup. The appetizer, floating in a rose-embellished bowl, proved rich and creamy. She felt full after she ate it and out of habit pushed back her chair to take the dish into the kitchen until the maid rushed over to retrieve it. She looked fearful of being reprimanded, giving Nash a sheepish look. But his benign expression told them all that no chastisement was forthcoming.

Being waited on made Becca feel odd and undeserving. At least the maid didn't make eye contact, in effect pretending she'd never seen Becca in the scullery. She would have to restrain herself so she could sit through a meal without rising to help.

Considerate as usual, Nash asked Becca about her brothers and sisters. The conversation lasted throughout the dinner, well past the promised lobster.

"How did you like your meal?" Nash asked after a dessert of cake drizzled with fig icing.

"Wonderful. I've never been so full. And I've never seen so much in the way of cream and butter in my life."

Nash chuckled. "Cook did her best to please, as you can see. Do you wish to eat meals this rich every night?"

The lavish meal had indeed been a treat, but she wasn't accustomed to so much food, and it felt heavy on her stomach. How could she tell him the truth without seeming ungrateful? She answered without looking up. "Uh, well. . .it was delicious, but I ain't sure I could."

"Good. I don't want to overindulge at every meal, either. We can eat more simply and save an abundance of cream and butter for holidays. I happen to like johnnycakes, for one." He smiled.

"Johnnycakes!" Becca restrained herself from jumping up and down like a toddler. The corn cakes, popular in Rhode Island, were a special treat at her house. "They're my favorite, too."

Nash chuckled. "I think you and I will get along just fine. Now, if you will, I'd like to escort you to the parlor for coffee. It's a little luxury I enjoy."

"Of course." She found the custom strange, but pleasurable, since it gave her more time with Nash. The next hour flew by for Becca as the clock chimed on the quarter hour.

"It's getting late, and I hate to see the evening end," Nash said as they lingered over the last drops. "I'll have Jack take you home."

"Home? But I thought I'd stay here with you."

"Oh. I hadn't considered you might think that." His eyes filled with regret. "If you were still my scullery maid, such an arrangement would be fine and good. But now that we plan to wed, I'm afraid tongues will wag if we share the same residence before our wedding day, the presence of servants notwithstanding."

"You didn't seem to care much about waggin' tongues when you talked about our match." Her disappointment made her tone seem more argumentative than she liked.

"I realize I might seem contradictory. Such is not my intent. It is important to me to protect your reputation." He turned even more serious. "I won't deceive you, Becca. Because we are worlds apart in rank, even with both of us conducting ourselves with the utmost propriety, there will be talk. You are taking a courageous step to agree to marry me, and I appreciate you for it. I hope you're not too afraid."

"No. Not with you beside me."

"Good. Go home now, and sleep well tonight. I'll send Jack over to collect you in the morning, and we shall continue our adventure."

❧

Later that night after she had shared the remaining food from the Abercrombie kitchen with her astonished family and told them about the evening, Becca tossed and turned on the mattress stuffed with straw. Fashioned for one, she nevertheless had to share it with her sister. Every once in a while Sissy, slumbering beside her, would tap her to discourage so much movement, but sleeping proved difficult as she relived the evening's events in her mind. Nash's advice to sleep well seemed impossible to follow. She couldn't remember the last night she went to bed with a satisfied belly. Conscious that the younger children should have enough, the older siblings and Mother had always eaten last, dividing between them the portions left after the youngsters had partaken. Never had she eaten until she couldn't eat more. Filled with food far richer and in greater quantity than she was accustomed, she could hardly breathe. She reminded herself that she couldn't eat as much in the future. But how could she waste a drop of such fine food? To do so seemed sinful. Maybe she could ask Cook to send out small portions for her.

Excitement didn't help. She could only think of her new life. Being overworked and the pressure Father put on her to provide money kept her from being completely happy all her life, but poverty never worried her. She had become accustomed to a meager diet and her mother's embarrassment of being unable to pay bills on occasion. Winter meant shivering in rags against the cold, even indoors. But in this neighborhood, most families lived the same—maybe a bit better off on occasion, but often worse. Not until Becca peeked into the homes of Providence's well-to-do did she see the gap for herself.

Nash came with his money, and she wasn't sure if she'd ever be comfortable in riches. Yet if he loved her as much as she now believed she could love him—indeed, already she had started growing fond of the kind and dashing gentleman— she'd do her best.

The next morning she rose, still tired but too excited about going back to Nash's to care. Donning her same dress, she hoped he wouldn't mind seeing her in it yet again. Surely the women with whom he grew up owned many ensembles. One of their everyday dresses must look better than her best frock. She tried not to think about it because there was nothing to be done.

She left the bedroom and found her father and brothers waiting for breakfast. Mother and Naomi scurried to prepare them a modest meal.

"What are ya doin' here among us?" Father asked as soon as he spotted her. "I thought ye'd moved in with that fancy feller o' your'n." His voice grew menacing. "Ya didn't spoil things, did ya?"

"Oh no, Father. It's only proper fer me to come home ever' night now that I ain't a servant."

Father nodded. "I hadn't thought of it that way. Ye're right."

"We had a good evenin'," Becca said. "We talked and even had coffee after dinner."

"That's why ya couldn't sleep last night," Naomi said. "Ya kept me awake."

"She kept me awake, too," Sissy added.

The other sisters murmured in agreement.

"I'm sorry." Becca looked at each of them in apology.

"What possessed ya to drink coffee at night?" Mother asked. "If we're lucky enough to have any, I drink it in the mornin' to stay awake."

"I hadn't thought about that. I'll try not to drink it so late anymore. Oh, but I was so excited I don't think warm milk could have put me to sleep last night."

"Ya did have an excitin' evenin'," Naomi admitted.

"Hey, wait a minute." Father grabbed her left hand. "Where's yer ring? Don't rich people give rings when they say they're gonna get married?"

Becca looked at her bare hand. Father squeezed it so tightly it hurt. "I—I don't know. He didn't give me one." She pulled her hand out of his grasp.

"Ya better do as I say and start collectin' those trinkets. This'll end soon enough." He nodded in a knowing way.

Mother changed the subject. "When are ya supposed to go back?"

"I think he mentioned somethin' 'bout pickin' me up today. I guess he'll send Jack."

"Who's that?" Willie asked.

"His driver."

The sound of horses' hooves could be heard just outside the door.

"Mebbe that's him now." Becca rushed to the front door and opened it. The Abercrombie carriage was parked outside. "Yea, that's Jack. I'll get ready to go now." She hurried into the bedroom to retrieve her coat and bonnet.

When she returned to the front room, Becca was shocked to see Nash. "Mr. Abercrombie!" She wanted to embrace him, but with her family watching in shock, suspicion, and awe, she thought better of it.

Nash, clad in a fashionable morning suit, stood on their doorstep. Though he dressed less ostentatiously than many in his social set, his suit showed him to be a man knowledgeable of the latest style and possessing the ability to afford an expert tailor. Wide-eyed stares from children and adults on the street trying not to look his way told her how out of place he appeared in the neighborhood. Waves of embarrassment swept over Becca, emotions that made her feel ashamed. Shaking off the feeling, she reminded herself that poverty defined her but was no sin. "Won't you come in?"

Instead of recoiling, Nash acted with the utmost politeness—as though he were one of them—as she made introductions. To her shock, he even presented each of her siblings a small gift—toys for the younger set and scented toiletries for the older ones. Though he had only spent his pocket change, Becca surmised he had no idea how much the day seemed like Christmas to all of them.

"I hope I might take this opportunity to speak with you, Mr. Hanham," he said after pleasantries had been exchanged.

Greed glinted in his eyes. "Clear out!"

His family scattered. Even Becca had to leave. She prayed her father wouldn't say anything to embarrass her.

six

Nash sat across the rough-hewn table from Mr. Hanham. Never had he dreamed that a man wearing tatters and appearing on the verge of drunkenness before the noon hour would be his potential father-in-law. But his fondness for Becca had grown in a short time, and he knew deep love for her could develop without effort. Gossip and ridicule were sure to follow when people discovered her background, but he'd meet the challenge. A loveless marriage would be a worse fate. And with Becca beside him, he feared nothing.

Mr. Hanham eyed a younger man who seemed to be near in age to Becca. "Stop combin' yer hair here in the kitchen, Elias. What's the matter wif ya? Fergot yer manners?"

Elias's puzzled expression told Nash that his father didn't usually reprimand him for grooming in the same area where the family ate.

"Run along now." Mr. Hanham's tone said he meant business.

Elias nodded. He was the last sibling to exit, so Nash and Mr. Hanham were left in relative privacy. Studying the older man, Nash could see that he must have been handsome not so long ago. Traces of Becca could be seen in his face, aged beyond its years thanks to poverty and hard drink.

"So." Mr. Hanham eyed him and took a swig of ale. "I understand ya want ta marry me daughter."

"Yes, I would. I beg your pardon for not consulting with you first, Mr. Hanham. I'm afraid my proposal was a bit impromptu."

"Imprompt—what?"

Nash searched for a definition. "Uh, unplanned."

"Oh. So how do ya make all yer money?"

Though the query was appropriate from a future father-in-law, Nash nevertheless tried not to reveal his surprise at the blunt way Mr. Hanham expressed himself—and so early during their interview. He cleared his throat. "I am in charge of the trading company I inherited from my father. My business is stable, and I believe your daughter will have a comfortable life."

Mr. Hanham indulged in a fresh drink of ale, looking at Nash over the mug. "So ye're really goin' through with it?"

"That is my honest intention, yes, sir."

The older man set the mug on the table. "Not that I blame ya. She's a mighty pretty thing." He wiped his mouth with his shirtsleeve, prompting Nash to notice a lack of table linens.

"Yes, she is," he answered with genuine cheerfulness. "But her spirit inside is what attracted me to her."

"Really?" Mr. Hanham picked up his mug.

"Yes. One fact that impressed me most about her was how important her family is to her. So you can see especially why I pray you can support and bless our union."

Mr. Hanham downed the rest of his ale, set the mug on the table with a *thump*, and looked Nash in the eye. "I know she's pretty, but so are those high-society ladies. What do ya want with a girl outta my brood? I may be poor, but I ain't stupid. I know what some of you wealthy types think you can get away with."

Nash held back a retort at such an insult, forcing himself to remember this man didn't know him as a person, but from rumors he'd heard from others about a world strange to him. If Nash were honest with himself, he'd have to admit some of the rumors about his cohorts were true. "I understand your concern, Mr. Hanham. I admire you for wanting to protect Becca. Yet if my intentions were less than honorable,

I wouldn't take the time and effort to approach you to ask you for her hand in marriage. In fact, I'd be more likely not to mention marriage at all."

"True," he conceded. "She told me ya asked. You're a rich man, and my daughter don't got no dowry to offer. How do I know ya don't plan to break off the engagement as soon as that woman nobody likes goes back to wherever she came from?" He crossed his arms and scowled at Nash.

So Becca had filled her family in on all the details about Hazel. He hadn't forbidden her to share, but the truth embarrassed him. Perhaps he should have asked her not to mention Hazel. He tried not to wince. "I realize why you might be suspicious, but let me assure you again that I am entering this engagement period with full intention of marrying her. If she'll have me, of course."

He laughed. "If she'll have ya? I'd think she'd be on her knees thankin' heavenly Providence fer lettin' her get the attention of a man as rich as you."

Nash was taken aback by the man's brash statement. The crude reference to his fortune reminded him of Hazel at her worst. He resisted the urge to retort, considering the family's sad surroundings. He kept his tone even. "I do hope I have more to offer her than riches. I have gotten to know her a bit, and we seem congenial. I have no reason to think that will change."

"Ye can't live on talkin'."

"True. I will provide for her and do my best to increase your comfort as well. Perhaps I might see my way clear to find a modest house for you. A house near mine so Becca can see her family every day."

His eyes widened. "Ye'd do that? Fer us?"

"Yes, I would."

"I'm not so sure I'd want to live in a fancy neighborhood. We're simple folk. We won't fit in."

"With the right education and changes in appearance, you could. I can help your children move up in the world."

For the first time the older man sobered, and his expression softened. "I didn't expect quite that much. Truth be told, I was just hopin' fer a hundred dollars. Guess that makes you a fool."

"I'm no fool."

"Fool or no, I'd say this calls for a drink." He summoned for his wife to bring Nash a portion of ale and to pour himself another.

She rushed in and hurried to obey. As Nash watched in awe of her speed, she placed an empty cup on the table.

"None for me, thank you," Nash said.

Mrs. Hanham stopped in midmotion, her expression taking on a resigned look. "Warn't there good news?"

"Yea, there was," her husband answered. "I told him we'd let him have our Becca."

The older woman's face lit, her cheeks growing to the size of small apples as she smiled. "Then I'd say this does call for a round of ale, Mr. Abercrombie. Don't ya want ta celebrate?"

"I don't need to drink spirits. My light heart and the prospect of marriage to your daughter are celebration enough for me." Making such a declaration aloud made Nash realize how strong his feelings for her had become.

❧

Though winter chill bit, Becca waited out front in pale sunshine while the two most important men in her life decided her future. Sissy and Naomi stood nearby, talking to each other since Becca hadn't entered their conversation. Their presence heartened her. Younger than Becca yet closest to her in age, they sensed when she needed them nearby even if few words were exchanged.

Familiar sights and sounds of her neighborhood floated overhead. One benefit colder weather provided was a lessening of the stench of horse manure and rotting garbage, though such odors proved inescapable in the best of weather. Most adults—and some children—worked in the factories or elsewhere during the day, so the streets weren't filled with whoops and hollers of happy games. The ragman pulled his cart, shouting about his wares, but Becca shook her head when he made eye contact with her.

What was taking them so long? "Father in heaven, Thy will be done."

As time passed, the chill made itself known through her coat. Shivering, she reached for the door just as it opened and Nash strode through it. His relaxed facial expression indicated he hadn't been too shaken by the encounter with her father. Becca caught a glimpse of her two sisters out of the corner of her eye. Naomi and Sissy pretended to watch a passing merchant hocking pots and pans, but Becca knew their ears were tuned to whatever news Nash had to share.

Nash glanced at the sisters and seemed to understand. "Are you ready to go home with me?"

"Home with me." The words sent a satisfied shiver down her spine. The idea that her home would forever be with him still seemed unreal—like a fantasy she had entered and would soon be asked to exit. But she didn't want to leave the fantasy. Not ever. Glancing at her front door, she wanted to point out he could stay for lunch, but with the Hanhams' finances in a pinch, she didn't want to put him in the position of pretending he liked the porridge Mother served.

"Yea, I'm ready." She turned to her sisters and bid them farewell for the day. They giggled and curtsied to Nash, a gesture Becca found both embarrassing and amusing. Ever poised, Nash tipped his hat to them and bid them an elegant farewell before helping Becca into the conveyance.

As soon as Jack shut the door behind them, Becca felt relieved to be in semiprivacy with Nash. Or at least away from her sisters' curiosity. Yet a little feeling of insecurity visited her, making her almost afraid to ask. "So ya asked Father fer his blessin'?"

"Of course. I said I would, didn't I?" His smile suggested teasing.

A relieved breath escaped her in spite of her best efforts to remain calm. "And give ya his blessin' he did, no doubt."

Nash settled into his seat. "Yes. He agreed after much questioning that we can marry."

"Questionin'?" She felt her face flush red. "How dare he ask anything of a fine man such as yerself. I'm sorry."

He leaned toward her and took her hands in his. Even in her distress, she couldn't help but notice they were the hands of a gentleman. Strong and manly, yet smooth. Looking at his fingers, she observed they were well tended, not rough and calloused like the hands of the men of her acquaintance. His fingernails were healthy and clean with no half-moon-shaped lines of dirt. "You have no need to ask my forgiveness. Your father's questions helped him earn my respect. If my intentions had been anything but honorable, he would have seen it, because his queries would have been hard for a man with ill intentions to answer truthfully. I know he's rough on the edges, but I think in his own way he cares about you." He gave her hands a quick reassuring squeeze and let them go. She wished he'd hold them forever.

Becca thought her father's real motives were caring about himself, but she decided not to argue. She lowered her voice and stared at the carriage floor. "He—he didn't ask for money, did he?"

"No."

"Good." She let out a relieved breath. The sigh filled the carriage, surprising her with its intensity.

"I want you to know I did offer your family a modest home."

She looked up and gasped. "A house? He asked fer a house?" Without thinking, she glimpsed outside and observed the homes they passed and wondered if he planned to buy one of those. Since the most insignificant residence in his neighborhood would far surpass their present accommodations, no doubt Mother would be grateful.

"No, he didn't ask for a house," Nash assured. "I offered it willingly. I hope you aren't too distressed about that."

"Distressed? No, but I'm not for sale."

"I know. I'm being a bit selfish, I must admit. I think having your family nearby will make you happy, and your happiness in turn makes me happy. You see, after we're married, I want you to see your family any time you like. I can see how much they mean to you."

This man thought of everything. She felt her throat closing as her emotions increased. "They—they do," she somehow managed.

"Your dedication to them increases your stature in my eyes. I've seen more of the world than you have, and you'd be surprised by how many people forget their families once something good happens to them or they gain access to a little money. It's as though they're ashamed of their relatives. I don't see you as having such thoughts."

"Never." She didn't have to pretend her strong conviction.

"Even better, I think the offer put aside any reservations your father might have had about my sincerity."

Becca didn't want to admit that his report of the interview eased her mind, too. With each passing gesture, Nash convinced her he was a man of his word. If it had been proper, she would have embraced him on the spot.

He changed the topic. "I told Cook we'd be content with vegetable soup and bread for luncheon. You'll find soup is my favorite dish during the winter months. I hope you don't mind that."

Though being in the carriage had dulled the winter chill, a bowl of steaming liquid to warm her inside and out sounded delectable. "I don't mind in the least."

"Good. I'm sure she'll have roast for dinner and no doubt fruit jam tarts as a treat for dessert."

"Everything sounds wonderful." Her mouth watered in agreement, though she felt guilty since her family wouldn't be eating so well.

"I want you to stay fortified. We have a lot of work to do."

"A lot of work?" She tried to envision what he meant.

He peered outside. "It seems we have arrived at our destination. If you'll follow me to the parlor, we'll sit and talk."

A nervous feeling hit, but the prospect of spending time with him in what had become her favorite room in the house cheered her. He helped her disembark, and they went to the formal room without delay. Becca took the chair she liked best and watched his movements as he sat across from her. No matter what his task—even something as mundane as seating himself in a chair—he moved with fluidity and grace, yet in a manner unmistakably masculine.

He tried to assure her right away. "As for the work I mentioned, I promise it's not as gloomy as spending your waking hours in the scullery."

She leaned forward. "What, then?"

For the first time since they left the Hanhams', he seemed uncertain about what to say next. He leaned forward and rubbed his thumbs together before looking her in the eyes. "Becca, may I be honest with you?"

As long as she could keep looking into his mahogany eyes, she didn't care what he had to say. She'd listen all day. "I hope ye'll never be anything else."

"Yes, but I don't want to hurt your feelings. Please try not to take offense at what I am about to explain to you, but it has to be said." He paused and took a breath. "I'm sure you realize you haven't been trained to be a lady accustomed to living a life filled with the finer things and mannerisms with which I am familiar."

"Oh." She looked downward. "I know it."

"The work I mentioned isn't work, really. In fact, I hope you can find pleasure in what I have in mind for you. It involves training you to be at ease among my friends and acquaintances."

"Trainin' me? Ya mean I have ta go to school?" Recalling repetitive ciphering, she scrunched her nose.

He chuckled. "Not exactly. I just want to show you how to conduct yourself in your new world, that's all. You can trust me when I say I am doing this for you more than for myself. I want you to be comfortable in my world and able to present yourself as a refined woman. We will start with your wardrobe and your manner of speech."

"I don't mind the idea of wearin' pretty dresses, but I don't know much about talkin' like a society person."

This time he didn't chuckle, but laughed outright. The musical sound broke the tension, and he relaxed in his chair. "You're smart. You'll get the idea soon enough. For one, be careful never to refer to riches or wealth. You must not appear to be self-conscious about having funds at your disposal. Doing so in our social setting is considered quite tactless and impolite."

"I—I think I can remember that." Her lips curled in a rueful manner. "We don't hardly ever talk about money where I come from either 'cause there ain't none to talk about."

He flinched but recovered with good grace. Becca wondered if his embarrassment stemmed from her sorry financial state or the way she spoke. Maybe both. "I'm glad we understand each other. Now, Harrod and I will be instructing you on how to form your words properly and how to speak with an expanded vocabulary."

Her stomach lurched with anxiety. "That sounds hard."

"It might seem strange at first, but you'll soon become accustomed to speaking as a lady should, and before you realize it you'll sound as though you attended a fine finishing school. Proper speech will become a habit. A habit you'll be so proud of you'll never want to break it." The warmth in his gaze seemed convincing.

"I guess."

"Better to say, 'I suppose.'"

"Oh." She clapped her hand over her lips. "I suppose."

"I have also engaged a voice teacher for you. Mrs. James will be by this afternoon to evaluate your singing ability and let us know how she feels about your talent. Hopefully she can teach you at least one or two songs so you can sing in front of a small group of friends. Informally, of course."

"Sing? In front of a group?" The idea left her with nervous queasiness. "But how come?"

"Being a lady means speaking and dressing well, of course, but knowing how to entertain at home is important as well. Fine ladies develop skills such as playing the pianoforte or singing. Sometimes both."

Her stomach jumped. "I just sing hymns with the rest of the congregation in our little church, and sometimes we sing old folk songs at home. I ain't never sung in front of anybody who really cared much what I sounded like."

"Hymns and folk songs are fine. She can judge the range of your voice based on those. Remember, she's there to work with you, not to be unduly critical or harsh."

"I ain't so sure. . . ."

"Oh, please do try. I think you'll enjoy singing greatly once you have a few lessons," he said. "I would have suggested the pianoforte, but I don't think it will be possible to have you proficient in any song on such a complicated instrument in time to entertain our friends."

Our friends. That sounded divine. Divine enough for her to decide to overcome her fears. "Then I'll sing as good as I can."

"As *well* as I can."

"Oh." She didn't care for the fact he had to correct her grammar, but at least he was kind and it was part of the lessons she had to learn. She wasn't sure she could have abided someone less compassionate. "As well as I can."

"Very well." He surveyed her appearance from the top of her head to the ends of her scuffed shoes. His gaze didn't seem critical, nor was it without sympathy. Still, she knew her mode of dress and manners had a long way to go to be considered adequate. Remembering that both of her soles sported holes, with a self-conscious motion she planted both feet on the floor so he wouldn't see. "We must address the fact of your appearance."

"Yea," she responded.

"Yes."

Couldn't she say a word that was right? "Yes." She suppressed an impatient sigh.

"As for your appearance, of course you already realize you cannot wear the same simple frock every day." His voice sounded kind, and his eyes told her he wished he didn't have to be so critical. "I thought you might enjoy an outing, so we'll stop by the cobbler's for several pairs of new shoes—"

Several?

"—and the milliner's for new bonnets and hats."

New bonnets and hats? He said more than one? Shoes, too! The shoes she wore were several years old since her feet hadn't grown in a while, and they were her only pair. Owning more than one new pair seemed like something out of a storybook.

"You look pale," he noticed. "Are you quite all right?"

She nodded so fast her head must have looked like a

bouncing ball. "I—I only hope I can be worthy to wear such finery."

"You are worthy, no matter what you wear."

"Well, if you'll have me ta look like a lady, I'd better sound like one. I'll work on me speech."

He grinned. "Better to say, 'my speech.'"

She clapped her hand over her lips again. "My speech."

His kind laughter filled the room. "You don't need to put your hands over your mouth when you make a mistake. You have nothing about which to be ashamed. Even the best of us have to learn proper speech."

"E—even you?"

"Even me." He grinned. "My governess, Miss Winters, had quite a time with me, but she made sure I learned."

"Was she as cold as her name?" Becca couldn't resist asking in jest.

He leaned toward her. "Even colder."

Becca shivered in an exaggerated manner, but bolstered him. "Oh, I'm sure ya were a good little boy."

"Not as good as she would have liked, I'm afraid." He changed the topic. "Oh, and I have wonderful news. I took the liberty of asking Harrod to hire a ladies maid for you."

"A ladies maid? Why, indeed? I'm perfectly capable of dressing myself, Mr. Abercrombie."

He looked at her attire with a studied eye. "First and foremost, now that your father has blessed our engagement and we can move forward, you must call me by my Christian name. And as for your toilette—if I may be so indelicate—of course you can adorn yourself in such a simple frock, but you'll soon change your mind when you see the buttons on the dresses I'm having made for you today. I may be a bachelor, but it's hard not to notice how many buttons adorn most ladies' frocks."

Buttons? Dresses? Ladies maid? It was all too much.

She had an idea. "Can't one of me—my—sisters be my ladies maid?"

"The thought did occur to me, but I'm assuming none of your sisters has experience as a ladies maid."

She didn't have to think long. "No."

"Please pardon me, as I mean no offense to you or your sisters, but I feel since you are new to this type of life, you need someone with experience. Someone familiar to this world who can give you compassionate advice," he said. "Harrod has just the woman. I have no doubt you'll like her. In fact, she will become your closest female companion, a friend and confidant to you. She worked for one of Providence's finest families, and the only reason she's available now is because her mistress, sadly, has departed this life."

"Oh, I am so sorry."

"Yes, she will be missed, but I am confident she resides in heaven now. We are blessed that the timing is fortuitous for the maid, since there was no other position for her in the family. Her name is Bernice Knowles. She's due to arrive tomorrow morning."

Remembering how Cook knew her family, Becca felt a bolt of unexpected fear. "Does she know who I am?"

He hesitated. "I did ask Harrod to fill her in only on the details she needs to know. My trusted butler and I would never consider placing you in the hands of anyone, servant or otherwise, who would do you harm. I assure you, she will understand the situation and will treat you with the greatest respect and courtesy. If she doesn't, you can report any infraction to me and she will be dismissed without question."

A different kind of fear visited Becca at this statement. She had never possessed the power to determine anyone's future, including her own. Her father had always decided what she would do and when she would do it, and she never interfered with the affairs of her mother or any of her siblings. The idea that one word from her could cause the loss of a job for anyone scared her. She wasn't sure she wanted that kind of power.

Obviously unaware of her anxiety, Nash continued. "Harrod will be instructing Bernice to help you stay on top of your speech patterns and any other little niceties you need to know. But if she is ever in the least bit impatient or harsh with you, that will not be acceptable and will be cause for her dismissal."

"Oh, I ain't plannin' to dismiss anybody."

"Perhaps it is better to say, 'I have no intention of dismissing anyone.'"

She nodded. "I have no intention of dismissin'—dismissing—anyone." Such elegant speech sounded strange to her ears, coming from her own mouth, but as Nash had pointed out, she'd have to become accustomed to speaking as a well-positioned lady would.

"See, doesn't that sound much more lovely?" he asked.

She nodded. "Yes, it does." Without letting Nash know, she congratulated herself.

"I told you you'd learn quickly." He became more serious. "After we marry, you can dismiss any servant you like."

She gasped. "I ain't—I mean, I'm not sure I want so much responsibility."

"With each feeling you share with me, I become more confident that I made the right decision to ask you to marry me," he said. "Only a person of character would make such a statement. Many other people thrown into your position so suddenly would be almost drunk with the prospect of lording their newfound authority over others. I can see you will be a wonderful wife for me."

Wife. Her heart beat faster at the prospect. Could it be true? She still didn't believe it. "I hope so."

"Not that I think you'll have cause to dismiss anyone,

at least not anyone we currently have in our employ. My servants have been faithful to my family for many years, and I have no reason to think you and they won't be congenial."

"I'll do me—my best. I don't wish to cause disruption. My father ain't—I mean, isn't—fond of work, but for the most part, I know how much people depend on their jobs." She swallowed. "So when do we get started on our work?"

"I can see we need to help you develop patience." His tone was indulgent, not reprimanding. He drew a small velvet pouch out of his desk drawer and handed it to her. "This seems to be the right time to present you with a token of my commitment to you."

She waved her palm toward him. "Thank you, but I can't take a gift."

"Of course you can. It's tradition. At least, it's tradition in my family."

Remembering Father's insistence that she gather as many jewels as possible, she felt too uncomfortable to accept anything. "It's not tradition in my family. My mother just has a thin gold band, and she didn't get that until her weddin'—wedding—day. That's all I'll need. Keep whatever it is in that box."

"Then you don't know it's a ring." His rueful grin tempted her.

"What else could it be?"

Nash shrugged. "It may be, and it may not be. Why don't you open it and see?" He handed it to her.

Deciding there was no other option, she took the box from him. Opening it she found a gold ring set with a large ruby flanked by a small diamond on each side. The idea that anyone would give her something so exquisite left her wordless. All she could do was try to fight back tears of happiness. "It's—it's beautiful! I wish I could take this, but I can't." She sniffled.

"Yes you can."

"No." She handed it back to him. "I can't."

He looked puzzled, then a flicker of realization crossed his features. "You're afraid if you accept it, I'll think you're materialistic, don't you?"

"Materialistic? Do you mean that I only want your money?"

"Yes. That's what it means, and no, I don't think you just want my money. Not for a moment." He paused. "With your permission, may I speak frankly?"

"Yes."

"Let me remind you that already there is a woman desperately wanting to be engaged to me—thinking she is engaged to me even though I never asked her to be my wife—and I have every reason to think she is interested in nothing but my money. But she does offer a pedigree and already knows what's expected of her in our social circle."

Becca winced.

"So think, Becca. Why would I propose to someone else I thought wanted nothing but my money?"

She thought. "I—I suppose you wouldn't."

"That's right." He touched her hand so that it seemed as though a butterfly had lit on it for the briefest of moments, then withdrew it. The gesture was enough to show her his growing feelings, yet assured her he planned to remain a gentleman. Her tension diminished as he continued. "I realize all of this must be overwhelming to you. You have left a world where you had to scrape for a morsel to eat each day and entered a domain where you can enjoy more than enough of everything you could want or need. Of course none of this feels natural to you."

"It don't—doesn't. I'm sorry. I'm such a fool."

"No, I am the one who shouldn't have rushed you by introducing so many changes in the course of a morning." He stared at the ring. "I should have waited before giving you Grandmother's ring."

She gasped. "Your grandmother's ring!"

"Yes. Grandmother Abercrombie wore this all her life. She presented it to me as long as I promised my future wife would wear it."

By now tears coursed down her cheeks. Even when she cried because of happiness, Becca wasn't prone to prettiness. Knowing her face must make her look like a bloated, overripe tomato made her feel worse. "Of course I'll accept it. How could I offend your dear grandmother?"

"I'm sure she's smiling down from heaven now." He took it out of the box. "Will you let me see your left ring finger?"

She extended her hand.

He slipped it on her finger. "How does that feel?"

The ring was a bit loose and the stone made it feel too heavy to bear, but she'd wear it no matter what. She nodded mutely as she stared at the jewelry, not believing it adorned her own hand and not someone else's.

"Wear it for a few days and see how it feels. We can see our family's jeweler to have the fit adjusted if necessary."

Too elated for words, she could do nothing but nod. She tried not to stare at the ring, the first piece of jewelry she had ever owned, as though she were afraid of it. Imagine, a fine man such as Nash Abercrombie trusting her with his grandmother's ring! She remembered her father's glee at the prospect of newfound wealth. He'd be happy to see her sporting such a fine ruby and diamonds, but the ring would always be hers.

Harrod entered the parlor. "Dawn Cobbs has arrived, Mr. Abercrombie."

Nash whipped his head toward the butler, refocusing his attention. "The seamstress?"

Harrod's eyes widened, and for a moment Becca wondered if he feared he had made a mistake. "Yes, sir. The seamstress you asked me to engage."

"Oh. Yes." His distraction told Becca he wished the interruption weren't necessary. She, too, wished she could put off the seamstress and linger with Nash. "Indeed," Nash answered. "Send her to the Blue Room and tell her Miss Hanham will be in shortly." He smiled. "I hope you enjoy choosing patterns and cloth for your new dresses. I think you'll need at least three to start."

"Three? That number seems extravagant."

"Perhaps it is extravagant for where you came from, but not at all for where you are today. We'll start with basic frocks for you to be presentable at home, plus one dress for finer occasions. We'll keep increasing your wardrobe at a quick rate and also as special needs arise. And they will. I promise."

Put that way, she could see why he thought three dresses would barely help her start. Images of parties, summer outings, and fine dinners floated into her head, making her both awed and anxious. She tried to concentrate on her awe rather than her anxiety. Unwilling to seem ungrateful by not responding quickly, she rose, and he followed suit. "I'd better get ready now."

"I shall have Harrod show you to the Gold Room so you can freshen up. Though I still don't think you should stay here overnight until we are wed, that can be your room when you need the occasional nap or to retire for relaxation during the day. If you don't find your bed comfortable, your dresser adequate, or any other accoutrements suitable, don't hesitate to notify the maid."

She studied his expression to see if he was teasing her. Surely he realized any room of her own would be a dream. Did he have any idea how luxurious she felt knowing she had her own bed? What a contrast to sharing a tiny mattress! His serious expression told her he meant what he said. Since he'd had more than enough all his life, maybe he didn't understand the impact moving into such a grand lifestyle had on her. She prayed not to become ungrateful or spoiled.

"And though I hate to rush things for you, try not to take too long, as Mrs. Williams will be here shortly to teach you the fine points of speech and etiquette. In the meantime, the seamstress awaits."

seven

For the next few days, Becca didn't see much of Nash. Instead she spent her time amid a flurry of ladies employed to wait on her hand and foot and to teach her how to behave in society. Becca felt undeserving, grateful, and overwhelmed. How would she remember everything they told her? The proper way to address important people. How to distinguish one fork from another. The difference between a butter knife and a fish knife. Sizes of spoons according to purpose. They instructed her to pace her eating so she didn't conclude any course before her guests. Dining slowly felt strange after years of chaotic meals at the Hanham house.

And learning new songs to sing! The teacher's method of unrelenting criticism discouraged more than inspired her, but for Nash's sake, she persisted.

Their continued efforts evidenced themselves most in her appearance. Bernice, the ladies maid Nash hired, proved her worth. As soon as they met and Becca saw her sweet, plump face and upturned mouth, she knew she could get along well with such a cheerful soul. Bernice had been born in a Boston slum, so she knew what it was like to come from humble circumstances.

"I started in the scullery and worked myself up to being a ladies maid," she told Becca during her first day on the job. "When I started with my first mistress, Mrs. Devon, my speech was much like yours. There's hope, Miss Hanham."

Bernice's reassurances comforted Becca, though no doubt her new maid thought they had much work ahead of them. Still, she sympathized with Becca and did everything she could to help her transition, which lessened the burden for them both. Not only did Bernice gently correct her grammar and speech, she made Becca look the part of the future Mrs. Nash Abercrombie. Though she always made a point of being clean, Becca had never spent so much time on her appearance. Bernice styled and restyled her hair for different times of day, and she promised that once her new dresses were completed, she would help her don the appropriate dress for each time of day. Bernice even sprayed rose-scented toilette water on Becca, a luxury she enjoyed.

As they got to know one another, Becca felt more relaxed in Nash's house. She wasn't sure she'd ever be comfortable as the center of so many servants' attention, but she tried to relax and allow herself to be tended by others.

When she wasn't being served, speech and music lessons occupied her time. Practice was a must, and sometimes repeating the same song over and over bored her, but rehearsing proved less of a chore than she thought it might. As for speech, she tried taking tips from the poetry of the King James Bible. Such inspiration helped.

The outdoors held its distractions. Nash had offered to teach her how to handle a horse, taking her to the country to ride horses he boarded there for hunting and pleasure. Even in the chilly weather, she found she enjoyed the lessons. After she became accustomed to the pretty dapple gray filly he chose for her, she relished the feel of controlling such a large beast, riding along with fresh air delighting her skin. Even better was the chance to spend time in Nash's company. Rarely did they gallop, so they could talk as their horses trotted.

They took meals together and spent time with one another each evening before she went home. Every day confirmed her growing fondness toward him, and though he never played less than the gentleman with her, she could feel his emotions toward her grow as well.

As time passed and her new maid grew familiar with Becca's hair, she experimented with styles until Becca found one she liked in particular. Curls framed her face, and more curls cascaded from the top of her head, touching her shoulders for a lovely effect.

Becca stared at herself in the mirror as she sat in front of the vanity. "Oh, Bernice! For the first time since Mother styled my hair for me to tell Nash I'd marry him, I feel beautiful. Only this time I'm enjoying the experience even better, for I am not as nervous." She couldn't help but pat her curls with a light hand.

"I'm glad I could please you, Miss Hanham. I am eager to see the complete picture once you are in a new dress. The seamstress will be here for your final fitting today, am I right?"

"Yes. I hope the alterations are such that I'll be able to keep them all today."

"Just wait until you see yourself dressed as a lady should. I expect you shall look as a young princess does when she goes to her first ball." Bernice let out a little sigh.

Becca giggled. "It won't be a ball gown. Just a morning dress."

"Just a morning dress? It sounds as though you are already starting to think like an Abercrombie."

Bernice's observations left Becca feeling mixed emotions. To survive in her new environment, she had to think like a woman born to society. But she never wanted to forget her beginnings. "Do I sound like a snob?"

"Oh, I did not mean to say that."

"I know." She patted Bernice's hand. "I don't think you could utter a bad word about anybody if your life depended on it. You know you can be honest with me. So how do you know I haven't let all these blessings I don't deserve go to my head?"

"That statement, for one. And I see you reading your Bible every morning. As long as you cling to the Lord, you'll keep a humble heart. And I know that's what you have because I can see it. I think Mr. Abercrombie can see you have a good spirit, too. You're beautiful on the outside, that's a fact. Yet I believe your spirit is the real reason he chose you."

"Thank you." Bernice's opinion had come to mean something to Becca. Nash had been right. The servants had been respectful of her—more respectful than she deserved—but Bernice had become an advocate and a friend.

Her ladies maid adjusted a curl. "You are improving every day in manners and elegance. It is time for you to look like a lady as well. You have much of which to be proud."

She looked back in the mirror. "But such an elaborate style. I hardly recognize me—myself."

"You will become accustomed to so many new things that sooner or later you will not even think twice about them."

"Do you really think so?"

"I know so. Why, think about the way you eat now. Mr. Abercrombie does not overindulge as they like to in some fine households in Providence, but the food is superior, indeed."

"Yes it is."

Bernice sent her a wry smile. "I daresay you don't miss the meals your mother makes out of what little she has."

"I can't say I do. I've been taking food home at night, so the family's diet has improved greatly."

"I trust Mr. Abercrombie has found a new home for your family, as you were telling me was his plan."

"Oh yes. There is one for sale now only a mile away bordering on our old neighborhood, and I do believe Mr. Abercrombie plans to buy it for 'em—them." Bernice delivered her the kind of soft smile that reminded Becca of her understanding mother. Becca would have to remember to speak with proper enunciation even when they were alone. "I do slip now and again, don't I?"

"You are doing very well. I am impressed by how much progress you have already made in such a short time."

"My most difficult challenge has been learning to sing. At least, that's how Mrs. James makes me feel."

"She's not known for a sweet temperament. However, you should learn much from her since she's an expert vocalist," Bernice assured her. "Many society people have taken lessons from her."

"I can see she's an expert. I just wish she'd be more encouraging." Becca stood and regarded herself in the mirror. "I look forward to wearing a dress that matches the hairstyle you fashioned for me."

"That time will be soon. And with the arrival of more dresses, you shall be changing clothing throughout the day so what you wear is suitable for each activity. In fact, we shall be spending most of our days together getting you dressed and undressed and dressed again."

"That sounds as though dressing consumes a great part of the day."

"That it does."

"I hate to impose on you to spend all your time dressing me."

"You never impose on a servant. That is something you must not forget. You must become accustomed to all of us waiting on you."

"I feel so lazy." Perhaps she shouldn't have blurted such a bold feeling, but with Bernice she felt she could be honest.

"That feeling will pass. And you'll soon become accustomed to heavier garments with some loss of movement," Bernice said.

"Loss of movement?"

"Yes. Ladies' dresses and intimate apparel are heavier and allow for less freedom. After all, menial work is not expected of them. Or of you."

Even though she hadn't lifted a finger in the Abercrombie residence since she had accepted Nash's proposal, she'd always helped Mother, so the idea that she would no longer cook, clean, or tend to others seemed strange. "I think I shall miss working."

Bernice laughed, her bountiful chest moving with each echo. "You won't miss it long, no doubt. Now go on and greet your fiancé for the noon meal. He awaits."

ॐ

Since he had arrived home from his office a few moments before noon, Nash slipped into his bedchamber to freshen himself. The room, painted a pleasing shade of blue and decorated so anyone entering would know it unmistakably belonged to a man, served as his familiar retreat away from his cares and worries.

Relaxing in posture, he splashed spice-scented water on his face and hands to wash away the grime from the street and ash particles ever present in the city air. A few strokes from his boar bristle brush with a carved ivory back, a cherished past birthday gift from his father, made his hair glisten. The process soothed away the cares of a harried morning at work and prepared him for light supplication to sustain him for the afternoon ahead. The ritual had become a fond one, even fonder now that Becca waited to partake of lunch with him.

Whistling "Saint's Delight" on his way down the hall, he slipped into his study to wait for Becca. A highlight of his day happened when she would emerge from the Gold Room and meet him so he could escort her to the dining room and they could partake of their meal together.

Today the seamstress, Dawn, would bring the three dresses he ordered for Becca to the house so she could see how they fit. He mused upon who was more pleased by the prospect— Becca or himself. If only he could defer his business so he could witness her face light up when she looked in the mirror at the finest dresses of her life. He didn't mind seeing her in the same tired frock day after day, but she'd no doubt feel more settled into her new role while wearing dresses that made an attempt to match her beauty. Not that any garment, even one fashioned from the finest silks and ermine, decorated with gems and pearls, and sewn with gold thread, could compare to her natural glow and the radiance of her spirit that enhanced her physical beauty.

He contemplated how much she appreciated even the slightest favor he showed her. Never did she expect special consideration, acting as though she never left the home in which she had been born. In a way perhaps she hadn't, since she returned to it each night. The discreet arrangement seemed to work. In hopes of quelling gossip, he had warned the servants and teachers against mentioning Becca's presence and progress until they were ready for her to be introduced to the larger society. Since they valued their jobs, Nash felt certain they had honored his request.

When she arrived at his residence each morning, a wide-eyed look still appeared on her face. The fact amused him in a most pleasant way. What a contrast this sweet young woman was to Hazel. To the manor born, Hazel never let go of her sense of entitlement and reminded others with each encounter, in ways both large and small, that she believed they owed her the world. He remained amazed by how Becca conveyed a sense of gratitude toward God for how He had led her to Nash—and Nash was convinced that's what happened. Some less fortunate women might have taken the attitude of Becca's father—that Nash should shower Becca with gifts so she could cash in and have a small fortune to show for her experience should the situation go awry. He felt certain Mr. Hanham didn't see that Nash discerned his attitude.

But Becca. She was such a gift. An image of her drifted

into his mind, much as a placid wave might wash upon white sand on a moonlit night. The picture made him much happier than any beach adventure. He took his seat in the chair behind his desk and closed his eyes.

So immersed in thought was Nash that he didn't hear Becca's soft footfalls as she walked down the hall toward his study. Not that she was easy to hear on the best of days since a thick runner carpeted the floor, but usually she didn't catch him in an utter state of daydreaming.

"Are you ready for lunch?" she asked.

He jumped a bit. "Oh. Yes." Looking at her, he saw she appeared different. He studied her to see if he could figure it out before asking her.

"Nash, you're staring." She averted her eyes.

"I beg your forgiveness. I—you look quite extraordinary today, even more extraordinary than usual. There's something different about you."

"It's my hair. Bernice styled it differently." She touched her fingers to an outer curl and pivoted. "Does it please you?"

His heart beat faster as he noticed her beauty. "Yes. Yes it does. Very much." He moved toward her.

"Do you think this will look nice with my new dresses?" she wondered. "Truth be told, I believe that's why Bernice fixed it this way today."

"Bernice is a very smart woman. I do think the style will do the dresses justice." He took her chin in his hand. "If I may be so bold, I was thinking about how no dress could do your beauty justice."

She looked at the rug and fluttered her eyelashes, but the motion seemed genuine instead of practiced affectation as he had seen many society ladies perform. "You flatter me."

"No, I don't. It's true." He held back the urge to stroke her stunning mane of curls. Clearly Bernice had worked hard on Becca's hair, and to disturb it would be a shame. He focused on her big, beautiful eyes, the refined shape of her nose, her full pink lips. She took in the slightest of breaths. Nash stared into her eyes and saw them grow wider. Though not a naive man, never before had he experienced the intense feelings of yearning that Becca's mere presence stirred in his heart. "I can resist you no longer, my darling." He drew her into his arms with more urgency than he intended, but she didn't seem taken aback. Soon he became lost in her warmth and drew his mouth toward hers.

"I don't want you to resist," she murmured.

When their lips met, the sweetness of the moment far surpassed his fantasies. So this is what love felt like! He wanted more. He drew her closer in an embrace and kissed her again, deeper this time. She did not refuse, but returned his passion.

In touch with each other's spirits as they were, they chose the same moment to break away, with ever so much gentleness, from one another. Though he suspected his kiss had been her first, when she looked into his face, her expression bore no shame but revealed only the most pure romantic love.

"I love you, Becca Hanham."

"And I love you, Nash Abercrombie. I have loved you since that first night I met you. Not because you saved my life, but because you were ever so kind to me though I could do you no favor."

"Don't you recall what Jesus said? 'Then said he also to him that bade him, When thou makest a dinner or a supper, call not thy friends, nor thy brethren, neither thy kinsmen, nor thy rich neighbours; lest they also bid thee again, and a recompence be made thee. But when thou makest a feast, call the poor, the maimed, the lame, the blind: And thou shalt be blessed; for they cannot recompense thee: for thou shalt be recompensed at the resurrection of the just.'"

"Yes, I remember that passage from the Gospel of Saint Luke, although never could I recite the verses with such eloquence as you possess."

"Father required me to commit the passage to memory, saying that our family must live by it. He was a great adherent of a concept that in recent years has been termed as the French language phrase *noblesse oblige*."

"Noblesse oblige?"

"Yes. Those of high rank or birth are obligated to treat those who are not as blessed with great honor, respect, and consideration. So for me to buy lucifers from you that night was no sacrifice."

She took a moment to absorb what he told her. A lump formed in her throat. "I'm grateful your father taught you to be so thoughtful of others."

"As am I. And of course you know that compassion toward others is a part of our history here in Providence. Who better to demonstrate the concept than Roger Williams?"

"Yes, the founder of Rhode Island Colony and our fair city of Providence." Wishing to impress Nash, Becca reached back into her memory to recall long-ago history lessons learned at her mother's knee. "He thought people should have freedom of conscience. But freedom also means responsibility."

"I see you have been taught well," Nash observed. "Oh, and that reminds me. We must find some volunteer work for you to do. What are your interests?"

She'd been so busy helping her mother and adding to her family's lean income that unpaid work had never been a consideration. "I'd like to volunteer, but I don't know where. There are so many people who need help."

"True. Too many people need help." Regret colored his voice before he brightened with a suggestion. "You have a heart for children. Might I suggest that you put your domestic skills to use making blankets for orphans?"

She brightened. "That sounds wonderful. I'll do it."

"We'll have you involved in my church soon as well. Come now, we must make our appearance in the dining room or Harrod is sure to investigate."

eight

Becca gasped with excitement when she saw the results of her new seamstress's work. "Oh, Dawn, this dress is absolutely stunning!" She stood still in her bedchamber as Bernice fastened the last of eighteen silk-covered buttons on the back of her new floral-patterned dress using a long hook made for the purpose. For the first time she understood why society ladies needed personal maids. She never could have donned such an elaborate garment by herself.

Recalling the costume Mrs. Gill wore during their interview, Becca considered in amazement her own attire even prettier. She lifted the skirt to examine the pattern and feel the texture of such elaborate fabric. "Are you sure this is a morning dress? It's much too fine to wear around the house."

"Even the Abercrombie house, Miss Hanham?" Dawn's sharp features softened at the compliment.

"Maybe even the Abercrombie house," Becca said, only half in jest.

Bernice eyed a gown made of a green silk reminiscent of fresh mint sprigs. "I cannot wait to see you try on the evening frock."

"With your delicate figure and refined features, you're sure to look like a princess," Dawn agreed.

"I believe I want to save the most luxurious for last. I'd prefer to try on the blue afternoon frock next." She took in the loveliness of the colorful wardrobe. "I'm glad you already had such beautiful fabrics on hand so I wouldn't have to wait."

"Yes, ma'am." Dawn beamed.

Bernice spent considerable moments undressing Becca down to her new undergarments and then replacing the morning frock with the blue outfit. As Bernice fastened more buttons, Becca could see she would be spending more time in her toilette than she had previously spent diapering the babes at home.

As everyone predicted and Becca hoped, the afternoon dress looked just as good on her as the morning dress. She tried to imagine changing into a special garment for no other reason than the fact it was after lunch. Now that the dresses had arrived, such a ritual would be a reality of each day.

Bernice picked up a pair of kid leather shoes with slight heels. "Please be seated, Miss Hanham, so that we might change your shoes."

Becca complied and gave over her feet to the maid. As Bernice removed the first kid leather shoe she already wore, Becca couldn't help but think it was much too good for daytime. Yet the cobbler had insisted they had been fashioned for that purpose. "I don't want to take these off."

Dawn and Bernice laughed as Bernice slipped heeled shoes onto Becca's dainty feet. After they had been delivered the previous day, she'd tried them on several times to practice walking in them. They looked better than they felt.

Her efforts to learn how to walk in dressy shoes were rewarded when she saw how well they complimented the elaborate evening dress Dawn had sewn for her. Noting the dress, she couldn't help but be pleased. The color was striking, and the neckline accentuated her frame and complexion and complemented her figure while maintaining a perfect degree of modesty. She looked the seamstress's way. "I love how you followed my instructions and wishes exactly."

"Thank you, Miss Hanham." Dawn glanced at her lap and back to Becca for approval. "Since you seem pleased with my work, would you see your way clear to ordering the other three dresses Mr. Abercrombie mentioned at our last appointment? If so, I would be ever so pleased."

Becca didn't hesitate. "Yes, I would. When shall we meet next?"

"If I am not imposing on your busy schedule, I can stay as long as you please. I set aside all afternoon, and I brought enough patterns and fabric samples to keep us occupied the rest of the day."

Becca smiled. "I can think of few better ways to spend an afternoon."

≥≈

Later, as the dinner hour neared, Becca realized for the first time since she'd set foot in Nash's home that she felt as though she belonged. Though clothes didn't indicate one's character, her new hairstyle and dress gave her a feeling of confidence, the likes of which she had never before felt.

Preparing to greet Nash after his long day of work, Becca felt nervous somehow, though she didn't know why. Of course he would love to see her in the dress. She only hoped the reality of her appearance now that she had transformed into a lady would live up to his fantasy.

Soon Becca entered the study so Nash could escort her to dinner. He sighed when he saw her. She looked into his eyes, noting how he studied her with an awed expression. "I never thought it would be possible for me to say this, since you have always been lovely, but I've never seen you more beautiful. You flatter that dress."

She felt herself blush. "You mentioned you like the color blue, so when Dawn showed me the fabric this color she had on hand, I thought you might like to see me in it."

He smiled. "The other ladies will be envious of how good you look."

Other ladies. Nash meant to compliment her, but instead his words produced an anxious queasiness, reminding her of how she felt the first time Nash suggested she would sing in front of his friends. If she could put off meeting his friends forever, she would. She knew the day she'd be introduced to them would arrive, but she'd kept her mind from it. She'd been enjoying the dream of being in Nash's world, alone with him and his doting servants. Training, purchasing of dresses, horseback riding, and other ideas he had for her were for one purpose: to make sure she could survive in his world. A world filled with others certain to judge her.

Waking up from her semidaydream state, she saw Nash staring at her, eyes widened with concern. She had to say something. "I—uh—I don't want anyone to be envious." The words she spoke were true. And truer still was her next utterance. "I just want to make you happy."

"You make me happy, my dear. Happier than I have ever been."

❧

Each night, unwilling to remain in clothes that would make her seem too regal for the humble circumstances of her birth, Becca put on her old dress and returned home. Though she'd worn similar dresses all her life, not until she had donned herself in luxurious clothes did she realize how scratchy the mean fabric felt against her skin, or the drab and worn condition of her attire. Bernice always looked sad when she helped Becca transform from lady to impoverished girl, but Becca held her head up and resolved to remember she had not always been so fortunate. She would never be ashamed of or forget from whence she came.

Her efforts to fit in with her old surroundings didn't keep her family and friends from noticing the difference in her manners and the way she carried herself. Fresh confidence radiated from her, and she knew it even as she embarked from Nash's carriage. One night in particular, a night saturated with the false promise of early spring that encouraged all to be out and about, she felt more stares than usual aimed her way.

"She always did ride a high horse," she heard one of her old rivals whisper, thinking she wouldn't overhear.

Becca clutched the handle of her basket containing food, focused on the front entrance of her home, and walked in a dignified manner straight toward it.

"I heard Micah's courtin' Susanna now," another hissed in a voice loud enough to be heard a block away.

She wished Sissy or Naomi were nearby so she could say, "Poor Susanna," with enough vigor to dispel any myth that she cared what Micah did. Instead, she smiled in a most unaffected manner and nodded toward them. Narrowed eyes were her reward. She stepped through her front door before the catty women could make new observations.

"Becca!" Several of her siblings ran to greet her. Though they shared a deep love that could never be broken, the food she carried held its own appeal. The amount of leftovers didn't fool Becca. It was an open secret at the Abercrombie residence that Cook had been told by Nash to prepare more food than needed so Becca's family could enjoy plenty.

Mother greeted her with a kiss on the cheek. "We sure been eatin' good since ya hooked up with that man o' your'n."

Becca had to concentrate on her speech when among her family. Listening to them made it all too easy for her to fall back into old patterns. "I am glad you enjoy the food I present to you, Mother. Cook is quite generous to prepare extra provisions for us."

Father entered from the back bedroom. "I thought I heard me a hoity-toity miss out here. Who do ya think ya are, talkin' like that? Think ye're better'n us? Yer own family?"

Such questioning would have left her quaking in the past, but Nash's love gave her strength. "No, sir. Please realize that I must speak in this manner if I am to please Nash. I thought you wanted me to please him."

Father's gaze shot, unashamed, to the ruby ring on Becca's left ring finger. "Any more trinkets?"

"No, sir. He has been spending considerable resources and effort training me to become a lady."

"Time and resources? Ya can tell me all about it while we eat. That food ya brung smells mighty good."

⟡

"The morning mail has arrived, sir." Harrod entered the study carrying several letters. "This is a certain indication your friends have discovered you're home."

Nash swallowed. He'd relished his time alone with Becca. Never had he rushed home from his office every day at lunch and each evening with such determination, but since she spent each day there, he was eager to return to his residence. Becca's poise and polish deemed her ready to meet his friends, but he wasn't ready to share her with anyone, no matter how innocent the capacity. He'd told Becca the ladies would be jealous of her, omitting that men would envy him. If only he and Becca could stay in their dream world untouched by outsiders forever.

Harrod's voice broke into his musings. "It is past time you resumed 'at home' hours, in my view. You have been devoting entirely too much time to business, and since your engagement, you have almost become a recluse. A popular man such as yourself needs to socialize with his friends."

"I'll get out and about soon enough. Winter is a good time to keep to oneself. Furthermore, I haven't been encouraging visitors yet for Becca's sake."

"The moment of truth is upon us. I hope she is ready."

"I think she is. Haven't you noticed her progress?"

"Yes. She has done very well. But is she ready to face Miss Caldwell and Mrs. Gill?"

"Let's hope so. For all our sakes."

Without further observation, Harrod excused himself. His

mention of Hazel and her sister was not a good sign.

Nash shuffled through the mail, looking for any missive appearing to be from Hazel. His body slumped when he saw his reward—a note written in a fine hand on cream-colored stationery. Hazel's hand. The note he dreaded.

He broke the seal of gold wax embossed with the letter *C* so he could read the message:

> *Nash,*
>
> *I trust you are well. I am in hopes your entire house has not come to ruin in my absence with no one to help you oversee the staff.*
>
> *My visit with my aunt here in Hartford is drawing to a close. I shall arrive in Providence on Tuesday and expect to see you promptly at seven in the evening. Laurel says we must move forward with great haste to prepare for our wedding day. She believes an autumn wedding would be lovely, as do I.*
>
> *Have Cook prepare lobster for our dinner, to be served promptly at eight thirty.*
>
> *Yours,*
> *Hazel*

He set the letter aside and let out a heavy sigh. "Lord, I pray Becca will be ready."

&

Becca sliced her fork into the last bit of white cake with fig icing. She had filled out a tad since arriving at Nash's, but not too much. Her assurance and ease at the dinner table made meals much more enjoyable than they had been when she first dined with him. Nash could relax, too, since he didn't have to correct her. Now their conversations focused on matters of importance. Nash told her most men didn't think women should bother themselves with business or politics, but he interspersed some tidbits about the world along with talk about interesting items appealing to the sensibilities of the fairer sex. She looked forward to their nightly chats.

After pleasant dinner talk, he turned serious. "Becca, I have something to tell you."

She stiffened. "Yes?"

"You will be going home later tomorrow night than usual. Be sure to let your family know."

A thread of excitement went through her. Perhaps he had something interesting planned. "Of course. You will be needing me here?"

"Yes." He cleared his throat and patted his mouth with his napkin. "Miss Hazel Caldwell will be arriving. I think it's time the two of you met."

Miss Hazel Caldwell. *Witch Hazel.* Becca shivered.

"You have nothing to fear," Nash consoled her.

"You could tell what I was thinking. I must be an open book to you."

"Your reaction is natural, considering our circumstances. I want you to know how proud I am of you. Your level of accomplishment is extraordinary. You are not the same person who knocked on my back door seeking a job."

Becca contemplated what he said. True, she didn't feel the same. Her speech sounded strange to her ears as she listened to well-formed words leave her lips, yet it sounded so much prettier and more refined. No one would ever hear her complain about her new wardrobe. The dresses had taken her from a sad gray mourning dove to a bright bird of paradise. She enjoyed wearing colors—colors that pleased her eye. Judging by the way Nash looked at her whenever she entered a room, she could see he found her new dresses pleasant to view as well. Then again, the kiss had changed so much. The new light in his eyes told her his expressed feelings remained true.

Time and time again, she relived his kiss in her mind, and

the memory became fonder with each reliving. He'd made no move to kiss her again. The fact might have made her feel insecure except he radiated love for her each time they spoke or shared any achievement, big or small. While she yearned for him, she appreciated that he treated her with respect.

He took her hand in a brief motion of comfort, then let it go. "Go home tonight and sleep as well as you can. I'll send Jack for you at three in the afternoon. When you arrive here, please have Bernice help you into your blue dress."

"I know that's your favorite. But. . ." She hesitated.

"What is it?"

"I don't mean to sound ungrateful, but if we are to start seeing your friends now, won't I need more dresses? Not that I mind wearing the same ones every day, but you said—"

"Yes, I know. And considering how I've spoken to you so often about wearing a variety of dresses, you don't sound ungrateful—you sound right. I'll contact Dawn and ask her to move faster on our latest order."

"Thank you." That matter settled, a sudden panic filled her about a different concern. "I won't have to sing, will I?"

He laughed, though in a kind rather than mocking manner. "Of course not. This isn't an evening soiree, but a dinner with an acquaintance." He leaned toward her and lowered his voice to just above a whisper. "If it makes you feel better, she won't be singing for you, either. You'll be missing a poor performance delivered with much more confidence than warranted, I assure you."

Whether he exaggerated to make her feel better or if he spoke the truth didn't matter; his levity encouraged her. She giggled, then turned serious. "I'm really not ready to sing for your friends."

"I don't expect you to be ready yet. But sometimes I arrive home early enough from the office to hear the very end of your lesson. I must say, you sound identical to a songbird."

He nodded to the maid, granting her permission to pour him a cup of coffee.

Under normal circumstances Becca would have protested his use of such hyperbole, but her embarrassment superseded modest objections. "You hear me sing?" She gasped, chagrined at the thought of entertaining an unseen but important audience.

"I don't mean to eavesdrop. It's just that when I hear you, I can't help but stop and listen. Neither can the servants. Even Harrod has complimented your voice to me."

"Even Harrod? Oh my, I must be putting on quite a show for the entire household." Becca felt a mixture of discomfiture and satisfaction in learning she had earned such high praise but hid her emotions as she shook her head at the maid to decline the caffeinated beverage.

"Mrs. James is pleased by your progress." He stirred two lumps of sugar into his coffee.

"She is?" Her voice reflected her genuine shock.

He poured cream into his drink, transforming the liquid to a mellow brown. "That's what she tells me."

Becca recalled her teacher's chilly instructions, never laced with approval. "I wish that's what she would tell me."

"Oh, she's a bit taciturn. The fact she praised you without my prodding is remarkable indeed." He drank from his coffee cup.

"Indeed."

"Yes." He set down the cup. "My dream is that we can perform together sometime soon."

The idea sounded like a fantasy. To sing a duet with him? No love song written could express how she felt about him. "Together? So you're a vocalist?"

"I wish I had such talent. No, I merely strum an occasional guitar."

"I learn something new about you every day. Perhaps after this visit with Miss Caldwell"—she shuddered—"you can play a few songs for me?"

"If she doesn't depart too late." A mischievous light glowed in his eyes. "I have a feeling she won't be staying too long once she sees us together. So please try not to worry about tomorrow. I'll be here as your biggest aficionado."

She'd learned many new words in recent days, but "aficionado" stumped her. His teasing grin told her he wanted her to guess its meaning. Asking what words meant could give away her humble background, and for Nash's sake she wanted to put on a flawless performance for Hazel. She made her best effort. "I'm glad you'll be there to support me, Nash."

"Perfect!" His smile grew wider. "See? I told you that you have no reason to fear Hazel."

She could only hope tomorrow would prove him right.

nine

The next day Becca noticed the appealing scent of beef roasting over the hearth. In anticipation of Hazel's arrival, Cook had placed the meat in a pot with assorted vegetables. The aroma filled the house, making the place seem cozy and inviting despite cold spring rain falling outdoors. Any other time, Becca would have relished the thought of such a delectable treat and anticipated taking leftovers to her grateful family. But the arrival of the unwanted guest left her with no appetite, even this close to the dinner hour. Perhaps a lack of hunger would serve her well. Eating large portions would make her seem unladylike and subject her to possible ridicule from her rival.

Rival. That's what Hazel symbolized to Becca, even though Nash had no interest in her. Still, she had a feeling Hazel would put up the fight of her life to keep Nash once she discovered Becca's presence.

She said a silent prayer. *Lord, please be with me. I wish Hazel no harm. Indeed, I want her to find a man who really loves her. And Nash doesn't love her. Guide me. In the name of Jesus Christ, Amen.*

Becca summoned her courage before she entered the study where Nash awaited. His glance touched her from the top of her head to the tips of her new shoes and back to her face. "I see Bernice styled your hair in the way I prefer. And your dress is perfect. I'm glad I spied you before the gentlemen of my acquaintance, or I would have risked losing you to a wave of competition."

"Never."

A knock on the front door rang all the way to the study.

"That's her." Nash confirmed Becca's worst fears. "Now please don't worry." He rose, and Becca followed suit. Nash stopped her. "Please wait here until Harrod or the maid sends for you. I want to see Hazel by myself first."

"Oh." As much as she'd feared and dreaded this moment, now that Hazel waited for them in the parlor, she wished she could go with Nash and get the initial meeting out of the way.

"I won't tarry. I promise."

🙠

"What took you so long, Nash? I was just getting ready to go upstairs to find you," Hazel said as soon as his feet hit the bottom of the steps.

"Greetings to you, too, Hazel." He couldn't help but think about his lack of emotion. No yearning to touch her prodded him. Even wearing a stunning dress with not a hair out of place framing a face everyone in Providence considered beautiful, she held no appeal for him. Instead, the feeling of a cannonball in his gut made him realize all the more how right he had been to choose Becca.

Eyeing Laurel sitting beside Hazel on the sofa, Nash held back a sigh. He might have known Hazel would bring her financier to hurry along the nuptials that no one but they were planning. Out of courtesy, he nodded. "Laurel."

"Nash," she volleyed with the spirit of a catapulted rapier.

"I wasn't expecting you. I'll have the maid set an extra place." He seated himself in the chair next to the fireplace.

"I thought I mentioned Laurel would be joining us," Hazel said without any remorse coloring her voice. "There is enough food, isn't there?" She turned to her sister. "I wouldn't be so bold in front of society, but since we are alone, I'll speak freely, Laurel. You know our Nash. Never wants to risk wasting so much as a drop of gravy. At least for once he has a decent fire lit."

"You can't expect a man to run a house properly," Laurel said. "You know ours would fall apart overnight if Mitchell were forced to tend to the staff and other household affairs himself. Poor Nash. He needs you, Hazel, dear."

"Indeed." She crossed her arms.

Spotting Harrod from the corner of his eye, Nash sent him a quick nod, indicating he should retrieve Becca from the study.

Hazel sniffed. "What's that I smell? Is that beef?"

"I do believe it is," Laurel answered.

Hazel twisted her mouth in a way that irritated Nash. "I distinctly told you to have Cook prepare lobster for us tonight. What is wrong with your incompetent staff? The first thing I'll do after we're wed is fire the lot of them."

Laurel placed a restraining hand on her sister's arm. "Now, now, Hazel. I'm sure there was simply a misunderstanding." She looked up at Nash. "Isn't that true?"

"No, it is not true. I know you wanted lobster, Hazel, but I asked Cook for roast beef. And it's a good thing, too," he continued over her outraged gasp. "If I had ordered lobster, we would have been short because I wouldn't have ordered extra for unexpected and uninvited guests."

"Well!" Laurel, in usual circumstances the epitome of icy civility, appeared flummoxed.

"Nash, apologize this instant!" Hazel demanded.

"Since you have been frank in your speech about my wisdom, or lack thereof, in handling my household affairs, I thought I should show you the same measure of respect."

"That's all right, Hazel," Laurel said. "He's clearly over-wrought from the prospect of your impending nuptials. Grooms can get nervous just as brides become jittery. But you are the perfect couple, so a little tiff over an informal dinner that will be forgotten by tomorrow is no reason to remain angry. When there is a dinner to be hosted here that will count, Hazel will see to it that nothing is omitted. So for now, let's forget our harsh words and enjoy our meal."

"Wise counsel, I must say," Nash agreed. "However, there is another guest who will be joining us."

"Another guest?" The pitch of Hazel's voice reminded Nash of a girl languishing in toddlerhood. "But I thought we would be planning our ceremony tonight. No stranger needs to be privy to our personal affairs."

"Oh, but she is not a stranger. At least not to me."

"She?" Hazel's voice betrayed a mixture of horror and suspicion. Laurel's eyes widened.

"Yes," Nash answered. "Would you care to meet her now? She's waiting upstairs in the study."

Hazel froze, then tried and failed to put a pleasant expression on her face. "I suppose I have no choice."

"Of course we would be glad to meet any relative you hold in high esteem," Laurel managed with a bit more civility.

Harrod, displaying his uncanny knack for perfect timing, entered. "Miss Hanham, sir."

❧

Becca panicked when she spied a familiar figure sitting on the sofa beside a woman she didn't know. Mrs. Gill! What was she doing there?

There was no time to give him the courtesy of an explanation. "I can't go in there," she whispered to Harrod. "Please don't make me."

"But you must. He has already asked for you."

"Make an excuse. Please," she hissed.

Nash spotted Becca and called to them. "Is something the matter?"

"Not at all, sir." Harrod gave Becca a puzzled look but without further ado escorted her in, and Nash, looking not the least bit vexed, introduced her to the two women. His identification of Mrs. Gill as Hazel's sister cleared up the mystery. Still, Becca wondered why Mrs. Gill joined them. Nash hadn't mentioned anyone but Hazel. Becca kept her composure, looking with reluctance at Mrs. Gill. Though the woman looked her up and down in the same manner she had during their interview, no flicker of recognition flashed over her features. She didn't wonder why. Her hair and mode of dress rendered her almost unrecognizable. Becca breathed a sigh of relief and took a seat in the chair across from the women. Nash sat in the chair beside her with only a side table separating them. She could feel the comfort of his presence and was grateful for it.

"Pleased to meet you, Miss Hanham." Hazel's voice sounded as though she felt anything but pleased. "And how is it that you are related to Nash?"

She searched for a truthful answer. "Uh. . .uh—we met many years ago, but have recently become reacquainted."

"So it would appear." Mrs. Gill looked down her nose at Becca, reminding her of their recent interview. "We know all the prominent families in Providence. Indeed, even in most of New England. How did your acquaintance escape us, I wonder? I would have thought we would have met you at one event or another."

Harrod reentered. "Dinner is served."

"Very well, Harrod," Nash answered with the verve of a man who enjoyed hosting. "Ladies, shall we retire to the dining room?"

The sisters exchanged glances, hesitating. Their reticence signaled a small victory for Becca, but the battle was far from over.

Silence ensued until they were seated and Nash offered grace. Soon the first course of a clear soup was set before them. As they ate they spoke of people, places, and events unfamiliar to Becca. Nash tried to steer conversational topics to those of a more general nature, but working together, the sisters ignored his cues. Becca had no idea how the women managed such a feat, but they seemed to have reached silent agreement that they would do everything they could to keep Becca from contributing to the conversation. She sat silently through the first two courses. By the time the roast beef arrived, her misery had peaked.

Hazel scrunched her nose to express her distaste. "I had really been anticipating the lobster I requested. Beef is such a disappointment, especially since we just had cold roast for luncheon today."

"I'm sorry we couldn't please you tonight." Nash's voice held not a shade of regret.

"This looks delicious nonetheless," Mrs. Gill noted. "I'll have my cook steam some lobster tomorrow night for you, Hazel." She cut into her roast, the knife sliding through easily thanks to Cook's skill in meal preparation. Before taking a bite, she looked at Becca. "Did you hear about Janette Jones?"

Becca didn't look at her, focusing on the food on her own plate. "I'm afraid not."

"Whatever the news is, I doubt I'm current on anything concerning Miss Jones," Nash quipped. "And I doubt any such news would be of interest to my guest."

"So you don't know Janette Jones?" Hazel's gaze bore into Becca. "Why, I thought everyone in Providence knew her."

"Oh, but surely you know the Danforths," Mrs. Gill prodded Becca. "Elizabeth is in a family way again. This will be her fifth child. Which reminds me, how many brothers and sisters do you have, Miss Hanham? Perhaps I have had the pleasure of making acquaintance with one of them."

"I'm in no mood for idle chitchat," Nash interrupted.

"Then you shouldn't have hosted a dinner party," Hazel retorted.

"But this gathering is much less intimate than I anticipated," Nash shot back. "Hazel, I would prefer to hear about your trip to Hartford. Do indulge me."

"Oh yes." For the first time, Hazel seemed disappointed that the topic had been directed to her.

"Everyone was asking after Nash," Mrs. Gill pointed out. "That is what you told me, wasn't it, Hazel?"

"Oh, yes indeed. I could tell my cousins in particular wondered why they haven't received wedding announcements." She looked sideways at Becca.

"Did you tell them they haven't received announcements because I never proposed?" Nash's tone revealed his impatience.

"But of course we have an understanding. We have ever since that night at the Harris's."

A hint of sadness shadowed Nash's face, and Becca could feel his embarrassment at having to hurt someone's feelings. As obnoxious as Hazel had proven herself to be, she deserved the respect of others as a fellow person if for no other reason. The fact that Nash felt that way about a woman who had made herself the bane of his existence heightened Becca's love for him.

"Of course you have an understanding." Mrs. Gill looked in a pointed manner at Becca.

"I'm sorry to disappoint you, but we do not," Nash said.

The sisters gasped, but Mrs. Gill recovered first. "Surely you don't mean that, Nash. Why, to break off the engagement would cause considerable embarrassment to you and everyone else."

Nash ignored Mrs. Gill and turned his face toward Hazel. "I'm sorry. I never wanted to hurt you or anyone else. But as I must repeat, a little embarrassment now is much preferred over a miserable marriage that will last the rest of our lives. Don't you agree?"

"Miserable marriage! How dare you!" Hazel rose from her seat with such a rapid motion that the back of her chair struck the mahogany sidebar behind her. She didn't even look to assess the damage, choosing instead to throw her pristine white cloth napkin on top of gravy-laden roast beef. Becca cringed. Her family didn't enjoy the luxury of cloth napkins, but she was no stranger to laundry. The Abercrombie laundress would not be happy when she discovered a greasy stain covering the linen.

Mrs. Gill laid a consoling hand on her sister's arm. "Now, now. Nash is just nervous since the wedding is upon us. There's no need to vex him or yourself."

Hazel didn't seem to hear anything Mrs. Gill had to say. An accusing finger pointed Becca's way. "It's you, isn't it?"

Unsure how to react, Becca let out an uncomfortable gasp in response to the accusation.

Hazel's eyes narrowed. "I'm right! It *is* you!" As she spoke, her voice rose in timbre. "You're the reason why Nash is backing out of our wedding. Why, I knew it was you from the moment I first laid eyes on you—you—you—trollop!"

Nash stood. "I realize you are overwrought, Hazel, but I will not tolerate my dear Becca being called such a despicable term by anyone and especially not in my home. She is nothing but the finest of women, and you would do well to follow her example."

"Follow her example? Why, I don't even know the woman. And I never wish to." Her gaze set itself on Becca's ruby ring, and her face turned red. "Nash, is that your grandmother's ring?"

"It is indeed."

"Then—then. . ."

"Yes, it's true, Hazel. Your guess is correct. It is time for you to reconcile yourself to facts." Nash's voice sounded colder than Becca had ever heard. An unpleasant shiver visited her spine. At that moment she wouldn't have considered changing places with Hazel. "Becca Hanham is my fiancée. We plan to marry this autumn."

Becca's heart beat at a rapid pace. Because of the other women's vexation, she suppressed a smile.

"Oh, so you think you want to marry her?" Hazel's features wrenched in anger, and she turned her wrath to Becca. "Regardless of what Nash tries to tell us, I don't believe for a moment that you're one of us. I'll find out who you really are, Becca Hanham, and when I do, I have a strange feeling that Nash won't be so proud to have you on his arm. Society won't stand for one of its own making a poor match. You will never be accepted, and Nash will no longer be welcome among the elite of Providence. Do you really want that? Do you really want him to lose everything—his prestige, his friends, his influence, and ultimately his business? Will you still want him when he can no longer afford to buy you this kind of life?" She swept her hand over the room to remind Becca of the finely appointed house. "Come along, Laurel. I have nothing more to say." With a lift of her skirts, she turned to exit.

Though Mrs. Gill seemed the stronger of the two women, she rose to obey. "Don't worry about us. We have been guests in your home many times and can see ourselves to the door."

As the women left, Nash remained silent, and Becca stared at what was left of her roast beef. Any other time she would have relished such an appealing repast, but the women had made the entire meal a nightmare. She clasped her hands together, hoping to conceal their quaking.

Nash covered her hands with his. "Don't let anything she has to say worry you."

"How can I not? We can't keep my identity a secret forever. And even if we could, I couldn't live a lie. Not even for you."

"Of course not. And I would never ask you to."

"But she said she'll ruin you."

"She may try, but she will not succeed. My positions in both my personal and professional life are secure. My family has run our business for decades, and while your background is humble, your behavior is impeccable and your character above reproach. I don't believe good businessmen would abandon their dealings with me because of you, and if any do, I am confident the Lord will send other provision. As for my friends, well, we may find out who they really are. . .together."

His words warmed her spirit, yet fear lingered. "But the embarrassment. . ."

He took her hands in his. "I won't promise there won't be talk and whispers, especially with Hazel fueling the fire, but it will pass and they will see that not to accept you would be wrong. Remember, we are Rhode Islanders and have a fine tradition of fighting for those whom others spurn. True, Hazel has shown by her wretched attitude toward you that some of us can be dreadful snobs. However, I believe once you start to mingle with people whom I hold in high regard, you will learn that most of us are not." A sad light entered his eyes. "Oh, I'm sorry this has turned into quite a bit more of an ordeal than even I imagined."

"I don't mind for myself, but this is only the beginning. I know you are a gentleman and you want to keep your word, but I think I should leave now. Let me go back to my home where I won't be a bother or threat to you. Hazel must have gotten the message by now. She's angry, but surely she sees she can't have you for herself. You don't have to keep your promise to marry me. I won't burden you." She meant every heartbreaking word. She'd anticipated meeting Hazel to be a dreadful event, but even the servants' nickname for the woman hadn't prepared her for such appalling behavior.

He took her hands in his and squeezed them. Their warmth consoled her. "Oh no, my dear. You are never a burden. If anyone is a burden, it's Hazel and her sister."

"I must admit, I can see why you are reluctant to wed her."

"*Reluctant* isn't a strong enough word. Being with you

only confirmed what a mistake it would be to take her as my wife. Even if you walked out the door this instant and never looked back, I still wouldn't marry Hazel."

"Really?"

He nodded. "You have brought me more joy in these few weeks than I have felt in my entire life. The more I see how well you conduct yourself, the more I respect you. Certainly tonight was a great test of how you behave when others are rude. You have earned a place at the Abercrombie table not because of your birth, but because of who you are. Why, I can even say I'm proud of who you are."

"Proud?" She could hardly believe she was hearing such words.

"Yes. Please say you'll still marry me. Together we will face Hazel and all her cohorts."

"Oh, Nash. With you I feel I can face anyone."

He smiled. "And now for our next step, in which I'll prove how proud I am of you. It's past time for your family to take part in our life together."

"My family?"

"Of course. Would they be agreeable to taking dinner with me next week?"

She didn't know what to say. Did Nash not realize that no one in her family owned clothing fit to eat at the Abercrombie servants' table, much less with Nash himself? She couldn't imagine them feeling anything but uncomfortable.

"What's the matter, Becca? Are you quite ashamed of me?"

"Ashamed of you? Of course not. I'm not ashamed of my family, either. It's just that I'm not sure how they'll feel about supping in such a fine home."

"They will be related to me by this time next year. I'm afraid they'll have to become accustomed to dining with us." He smiled. "Would you like me to send several seamstresses to your house to sew them some dinner clothes? Perhaps being dressed for dinner will make them feel more at ease."

Becca held back her thought that her father would rather have a pitcher of ale from the tavern than a new suit from the haberdasher. But Mother—she would enjoy such a dinner. And for her sisters, the occasion would be nothing less than the fulfillment of a fantasy. Her brothers—well, they would enjoy a feast of plenty. "That is very kind of you. I'll mention it tonight when I go home."

ten

Back at her house later that night and donned once again in her plain housedress, Becca felt nervous as she served her father and the oldest boys at the Hanham table. Hazel's visit had set their dinner hour quite late. Still, her family didn't complain. Becca and her mother plus the girls and small boys would eat in two more shifts after the men. At least now that she knew Nash, their main meals no longer consisted of thin gruel and ale. With better quality food from the Abercrombie kitchen, mealtimes had become a source of enjoyment rather than dull routine. She couldn't help but contrast their present way of life to Nash's and felt grateful to him for the fact they would soon be moving to better quarters.

Becca made sure to give Father an extra portion of ale to put him in a good mood. She waited until her older brothers threw dinner down their gullets and hastened out to whatever mischief awaited them on the darkened streets and her sisters occupied themselves with chatter and chores. Tired after another long day, complicated by the burdens of an advancing pregnancy, Mother plopped back into her seat at the table.

Becca sat in the chair across from Father as he enjoyed robust swigs of alcohol. "Father?"

He gave her a sidelong glance. "What is it, girl?"

"My fiancé has asked if I can bring my family to dinner at his house next week."

Father set down his mug. "Did he, now? If the leftovers you've been bringin' are any clue, we'll be eatin' high on the hog that night, eh?"

Mother's expression revealed her discomfort and slight alarm as she touched the sleeve of her dress. "But what will we wear?"

"Nash has already thought of that. He'll have new clothes made for all of you."

Mother gasped. "New clothes! Why, with the number of us here that will cost a fortune. Are ya sure he wants to do such a kind thing?"

Becca embraced her mother. "Yes, I am. That's the thoughtful type of man he is, Mother. Always wanting to do the compassionate thing. You'll love your new dinner clothes."

"Dinner clothes?" Father spat out the words. "So he's sayin' our regular clothes ain't good enough fer 'im."

"They aren't." Becca tried not to sound grumpy.

"I don't care who he is. He can take us just the way we are. I ain't wearin' no dress-up clothes fer nobody."

"Ya wanted the riches and new house he promised," Mother argued. "Ya got to take the bitter with the sweet, as they say. A suit won't hurt ya none. Not fer one night."

"It's a waste, I tell ya. I won't wear it again." Father snorted and took a swig of his drink.

"You can wear it to the wedding," Becca suggested. "Oh, please, Father, let him buy everyone new clothes. You'll feel much more comfortable in a nice new suit sitting at his dining table. Really you will."

"Kinda like you feel more comfortable in all them fancy dresses he bought ya."

"No. . ."

"I've seen how ya show off to all yer sisters. All of ya squeal like little girls at the sight of blue silk." Father took another swig of ale and scowled. "He thinks he's too good fer us, but since ye've hit a pot o' gold, I'll swallow me pride and put up with it."

She wished her parent could have been more gracious, but

his ungrateful attitude was the best for which she could hope from him. "Thank you, Father. Nash and I will speak with the seamstresses tomorrow and schedule a time for you to be fitted. We think it's best if you go to her. He'll send a carriage tomorrow to pick up you and the boys. The next day, Mother and the girls will go."

"I just don't like it," Father argued. "Sounds to me like he's tryin' to make us some society types. We ain't. And I don't want to be. Why can't he just give us the house and let us live like we want? Did ya ask him fer money like I asked ya to?"

Becca swallowed. Though standing up to her father would never be easy, knowing Nash had made her stronger. "I don't mean to disobey, but I shouldn't ask for money. I just don't feel right about it. Don't you know he wants to discourage a society woman who wants his money? Besides, I'd marry him even if he lived right next door and didn't have a dime."

&

"Are you quite ready to go to the milliner's, my darling?" Nash asked the following day.

Becca looked forward to seeing what type of hats Miss Dawkins had created for her. "Yes, I am."

He peered out the window. "Well, we have a glorious, sunny day for our errand. Life can't get much better, can it?"

Becca had to agree.

He turned and made his way toward her, the motion stirring the appealing scent of bay rum spice he always wore. "Only, my life will be at a climax on the day we wed."

"As will mine," she agreed. "And I hope each day afterward I can only make your life better and better."

Taking both of her hands in his, he answered, "I anticipate you shall, my darling." He kissed the back of each hand and squeezed them before letting go. "Come, let us take the carriage now."

"Now?"

"Yes, is that quite all right?"

"Of course. I just wasn't expecting to leave so soon. Shall I don my coat?"

"A fine idea. A nip of winter still permeates this fine spring air." He inhaled deeply. "But speaking of your outer wrap, I've been negligent in taking care of you. It's past time for you to have outer garments sewn. Two, in fact. One for spring and one for winter."

She nodded. The standing wardrobe in the Gold Room was becoming full.

The ride to the milliner's allowed her enough time to catch Nash up on the news. "Oh, and I did speak with my family about the dinner. They'll be happy to see Dawn and the other seamstresses about clothing. Or perhaps I should say, Mother and my sisters are happy. I can't promise my male relatives are just as eager."

He chuckled. "Women's clothing is lovely and colorful, while we men are forced into dull colors and starched collars. No wonder they're not eager."

She smiled. "Thank you for understanding. So much has happened to me—to all of us—in such a short time."

"I know. With God's grace, we'll soon understand each other completely." The carriage stopped in front of the shop.

"I'll take this opportunity to go to the dry-goods store for Harrod, sir." Jack jumped off the conveyance.

"Very good. But do be back in due time. Don't keep me waiting as you did last week."

"Yes, sir." Jack sent him a sheepish look before he vanished.

"He seems to be in a hurry to run that errand," Becca couldn't help but notice good-naturedly.

Nash's lips thinned. "I do believe he has his eye on the shop girl. He's a good driver for the most part, but sometimes he gets too distracted by his personal affairs to pay proper attention to his work. Years ago my father promised his mother we'd take of him, so I hate to let him go."

"It's hard to control a love-struck man. I've seen that look in my brother's eyes. You might have a wedding in your household soon."

"Another one? Indeed." Nash smiled and jumped out then extended his hand to help her disembark.

Caught up in her world with Nash, she took his hand, grateful for the excuse to make the slightest contact, and smiled at him. He looked into her eyes. Getting lost in his gaze, she almost missed her step, but managed to retain her composure. She could look in his eyes forever. . . .

The tip of her toe had no sooner hit the street than she heard the horrifying scream of a woman from the direction of a nearby bank. She remembered Nash mentioning a rash of robberies. Surely they hadn't stumbled onto the scene of a crime!

A man ran out of the bank and looked in both directions. Despite Becca's unspoken prayer that he wouldn't head in their direction, he did. Gunshots followed, gashing the air.

"Get back in the carriage. Now!" Nash insisted.

She turned to jump back in but moved too late. Without warning, a hand gripped her arm, ripping her from Nash's hold. Another scream followed amidst more gunfire. One bullet flew so close, Becca heard it whiz by. She let out her own scream.

The robber's grip wasn't the comforting hold of Nash, but a rough vise.

"Unhand her!" Nash demanded.

Ascertaining that Becca's escort was unarmed, the robber ignored Nash's demand. Instead, he kept her in front of him to discourage more gunshots from being fired in his direction. Before she could shout again, he forced her to mount the horse with a rude motion, then whipped up behind her.

"No!" Nash cried.

The robber responded by shooting once in Nash's direction. Nash ducked to avoid being hit. Becca screamed and reached for the gun to take it away from the criminal.

He wrestled his arm away from her while keeping hold of the bridle. "Try that again and I'll shoot ta kill."

Looking back well into the distance, she saw Nash pursuing them on foot. Even as strong as he was, Becca knew he had no hope of catching them. She loved him all the more for trying. The evil look on the robber's face told her he would stop at nothing to escape. At that moment she resolved not to interfere with her captor's intent, fearful that he would keep his word and Nash would be shot and fall dead before her. The idea brought a storm of tears to her eyes. Unencumbered, trails of hot, salty water streamed down her cheeks.

Winded, Nash stopped and waved. "I'll find you, Becca! I love you!" he shouted as the horse galloped into the unknown.

❧

Watching the horse rush away with his Becca, Nash felt embarrassed and helpless. If only he could have caught up with them! Why did he have to lose his head and run instead of jumping into his carriage and giving chase with the horse?

His fiancée had endured the dangers of poverty and its accompanying hardships all her life, yet with money and position behind him, he couldn't even protect her during a routine trip to the milliner's. Then again, despite being aware that robbers were about in town, he still hadn't expected to meet one—and be shot at, no less.

At that moment Jack pulled up in the carriage. "Shall we give chase, sir?"

Nash nodded. "We can try." He jumped aboard and held on as the conveyance made haste. Though Jack ran the horses as fast as he could, they were no match for the unencumbered horse they pursued.

"We lost him, sir," Jack admitted after several miles.

Upset, Nash had to agree. "I suppose if I hadn't lost my head and tried to run after the horse on foot, we might have had a chance. Go back to town. We must notify the police."

"Yes, sir." Jack urged the horses on, quickening the pace. Once they returned to the scene of the crime, they found police questioning witnesses.

An older woman pointed at Nash. "They run off with a lady what was with him."

A detective looked Nash up and down. "Is this true?"

" 'Course it's true," the woman protested. "I saw the whole thing."

Nash nodded. "I wish it weren't true, but he took my fiancée, Miss Becca Hanham, hostage and made off with her. Officer, you must do something. You've got to save her. She's everything to me." Though he had professed his love to Becca with every bit of sincerity he possessed, the fact that she could be lost to him forever made him realize the depth of emotion he had developed for her. He recalled her sweet kiss on his lips. What he would give to have her close once more!

"Slow down, sir," the officer urged. "What's your name?"

"Nash Abercrombie."

He blanched. "Oh. I'm sorry, Mr. Abercrombie. I didn't know. Of course we'll do anything we can to assist you. . . ."

"I don't ask for any more consideration than you'd give any other citizen. I just ask that you do everything you can to find her. He—he used my Becca as a hostage." Nash choked on the words. Not one to show emotion and never one to blather, Nash felt tears threaten. He couldn't let anyone see him like this. They might think him less of a man. "My driver and I pursued him to the outskirts of town before we lost him."

"Tell me as best as you can, sir. I know you must be shaken. They said the robber shot at you."

"Yes." Trying not to think about that part of the adventure, Nash related the horrible events and described the robber as a bulky man with dark hair.

The officer made notes. "Yes, that matches the description of one of the bandits. Lately they've been working solo. We'll find them all and bring them to justice. That's a promise, Mr. Abercrombie."

Wishing he could do more, Nash boarded the carriage and went home. All the while, he wallowed in self-doubt. If he hadn't brought Becca into his world, she would have avoided being snatched. He, not she, should be with the kidnappers.

"Lord, deliver her safely into my arms. I don't know what I would do without her."

❧

A repulsive laugh bellowed from the lips of the robber who had taken Becca hostage as he looked over his shoulder. "We lost 'em."

Becca's heart plummeted. Why didn't someone—anyone— from town catch up to them? She prayed all hope for her release wasn't lost. Fright seized her and wouldn't let go. Father's worst temper tantrums and outbursts didn't compare to feeling so alone. At least at her house her mother would try to protect her. She had no such ally on a galloping horse ridden by a stranger, heading out of Providence to who knew where? Never had she seen this part of the country, so trying to remember where she went seemed impossible. All she caught sight of was a marker for Meeting Street. Perhaps that tidbit would help in the future.

She couldn't help but wonder if Hazel, or someone connected to her, hired the man to kidnap her, but since she didn't know their comings and goings, misfortune seemed more probable. The man brought the horse to a trot. She sat in front of him with his arms around her, but they didn't comfort her. Being near such a man left her sick. "You've gotten what you want from me. I protected you from getting shot. Will you let me go now? I'll walk back into town myself."

"Let ya go? But I'm not finished with ya yet."

Her stomach lurched. What could he mean? She whispered, "Lord, I pray Thee will keep me safe."

"Shut up with prayin'," he hissed. "It's enough to give a man a headache."

Surprised that he heard her, she swallowed. Fear kept her from disobeying, but no one could keep her from petitioning the Lord silently. She prayed.

Soon she eyed a small log cabin near a churchyard at the end of a lonely country path. That must be where he was taking her. She couldn't help but note the cemetery. Would they kill her and bury her there in an unmarked grave? Or throw her unprotected corpse on top of some other poor soul's and cover them both with dirt? Anxiety clutched at her midsection.

Lord, I pray this isn't the last time I see the outdoors.

With a rough motion, the heavyset man pulled her off the horse and set her on the ground. Taking her by the hand without ado, he escorted her to the house, opened the thick wood door, and pushed her into a small room with tiny windows, lit only by two anemic candles. Becca's eyes adjusted quickly, and she saw two women and a man.

The first woman, a brunette with few wrinkles on her face but telltale grays in her hair, rose from her seat. "What took so long?"

The man had a question, too. "Did ya get a good take?"

A younger woman with a plump figure and ash blond hair jumped and ran to him, throwing her arms around him. "Dolph, I thought you'd never come back. I—I thought you might have been killed."

For a flash of an instant, Becca felt sorry for the blond. How would she feel if she were waiting for Nash, worried that something terrible happened to him? But then, Nash was neither a bank robber nor a kidnapper. . . .

Becca expected Dolph to console his female companion, but instead he grunted and made his way to the nearest wooden chair.

"What have we got here?" The brunette had noticed Becca and stared at her. Becca cut her glance to the blond, whose slitted eyes and folded arms revealed she considered Becca a threat. Becca looked at the floor in hopes of showing her that Dolph was safe from her affections.

"What does it look like I've got here?" Dolph sneered.

"We weren't supposed to bring a woman in the picture," the brunette said. "Have you gone mad?"

"Maybe I have, and maybe I haven't." As Dolph shrugged, the angle of his face in the light revealed he needed to shave his dark whiskers. "I grabbed her without thinkin' since she was the only woman around. Then, at first, I thought she was from the poor side of town, what with that old coat. But look underneath at this dress." He gave Becca's sleeve a tug that threatened to ruin Dawn's expert sewing. She tried not to flinch or pull away, fearful of inciting an unwelcome reaction from her captor. "She's got money, this one has. Isn't that right, Mac?" he asked the man.

"Yea," agreed Mac, nondescript except for an acute slimness of frame.

"You should of seen the man she was with. He was wearin' clothes good enough to see President Polk."

"So she was with someone?" the blond asked, looking into Dolph's face.

"Who cares?" the brunette asked. "We don't need her here."

"We needed her when they was shootin' bullets at me," Dolph said. "If it hadn't been for her, I might be dead sure enough." He looked Becca over as though she were a prize.

"Somebody will pay dearly to get this girl back. Don't ya think?"

The elder woman nodded. "Mebbe so."

"Who are ye?" Dolph asked.

The brunette woman surveyed her. "She looks mighty familiar. Like I should know her."

"Quiet. Ya don't know no high-society women." Dolph turned to Becca. "Now who are ye?"

Praying she didn't put Nash in danger by telling the truth, she put on a braver front than she felt.

She tilted her head high. "I am the fiancée of Nash Abercrombie."

eleven

Distraught beyond expression, Nash returned to his house to wait for news. He shared the story with Harrod, who soon brought tea to Nash in his study as comfort. Nash let the tea grow cold as he paced back and forth. He debated sending Jack to let Becca's family know what happened, but thought better of it. Such terrible news would best be delivered by himself in person. After all, he'd gotten her into the situation by bringing her into his world. Losing Becca would devastate her family, particularly her mother and her sisters Naomi and Sissy. Perhaps Becca would have been better off had he left her alone. But he could not imagine life without her.

"I'll wait two hours, and if there's no word, I'll venture out to tell them," he muttered. "Lord, I know we are to wait for Thy time, but I pray that in this instance, Thy time is mine."

Harrod knocked. "Forgive me for the interruption, but the newspaper published an extra today, sir. I thought you would want to see it." He handed the paper to Nash.

"Thank you, Harrod. You are dismissed." He sat at his desk and devoured the account of the daring escape and kidnapping. His name and Becca's appeared, along with the details. He groaned, thinking about the gossip sure to ensue. Of course no reporter would write an account of a robbery gone wrong, along with gunshots and an impromptu kidnapping, without publishing their names.

Once again, Harrod knocked. "Otto Blevins to see you, sir."

Nash was in no mood to see anyone. Already the police had been by to question him about receiving a ransom note. So far, he had not. "With my apologies, tell him I am indisposed at present and will see him another time."

Harrod's mouth tightened, but otherwise he remained unruffled. "Shall I tell everyone else the same?"

"Yes." He rubbed his chin. "Just how many people are there?"

Harrod placed several calling cards on the corner of Nash's desk. "As you can see, because of the newspaper's extra, many of your friends have stopped by inquiring about your health. They are concerned. Of course, I gave them no further details."

"If any more stop by, tell them I am well and will see them soon."

"I'll do my best to keep them at bay, sir." Harrod shook his head and left the study.

His exit left Nash alone with his thoughts. He stared out the window to a cloudy day. When would the kidnapper return Becca, or at the very least, send a ransom note? Why didn't God answer his prayers and grant her return?

Again, Harrod knocked.

"I told you I don't want to see anyone," Nash snapped.

"Yes, sir. However, I would not interrupt if I didn't feel, in my judgment, it wasn't necessary."

"Of course. I'm sorry. I don't mean to be harsh. I'm in a foul mood."

"You have every right to be," Harrod agreed. "Again, I would not have dared interrupt, only I feel certain you will want to see Miss Hazel Caldwell."

"Hazel? Did she say what she wanted?" He knew she was angry, but he didn't expect her to show up at that moment.

"She said she has a letter you will want to read."

"A letter?" His curiosity was piqued, especially since he knew Hazel wouldn't bother unless the matter really was of the utmost urgency. "Very well. Escort her to the parlor, and have the maid send in tea."

Soon he entered the parlor. They wasted little time in

exchanging pleasantries. Hazel carried a copy of the extra edition with her. She folded it to reveal the article about the events. "This is a disgrace! Being seen in public with this woman." Her nostrils flared with anger. "I have many friends in this town, and it didn't take me long to find out the real identity of your so-called fiancée. Imagine, trying to pass her off as a respectable woman. Really, Nash, have you taken leave of your senses?"

"I have not. Hazel, I am in no mood to discuss your opinion about my fiancée. As you can see for yourself in the newspaper account, she has been kidnapped. I am frantic with worry, and I await word from her kidnapper. I fully expect to be asked for a ransom. A ransom I will gladly pay to have her safe in my arms again."

"You—you really have become—fond of her, haven't you?" Her mouth slackened, and hurt evidenced itself in Hazel's voice. For a moment Nash could almost feel sorry for her. Almost.

"I love her," he proclaimed without wavering.

"You love her?" she sneered. "The idea of you even thinking of marrying her is a disgrace to everyone in Providence." She threw the paper on the tea table, almost hitting the pot full of hot beverage. Ignoring the near mishap, she folded her arms and faced him. "Now, I'm aware that you men sometimes indulge in, shall we say, little indiscretions. We women understand, and I can forgive you—"

"How dare you!" If Hazel had been a man, he would have been tempted to say something stronger.

She winced but did not apologize.

He stood his ground. "I assure you, I have no intention of conducting myself in such a way. While of course I am not perfect, I do try to live by God's commandments."

"Really?" she huffed. "Surely you have no intention of wedding that little back-alley girl. Why, how can you even look twice at someone who not so many years ago sold matches on the street corner? I understand she was even your scullery maid. You must think this is a joke, although it's not in the least bit funny."

"It's no joke, Hazel. Unlike you, I look at the person's heart. Of course, the fact she's beautiful to behold is a blessing." He smiled at the thought of his Becca. "And she wasn't a scullery maid for even a day."

Her voice hardened, lowering in pitch. "Ten minutes or ten years—it doesn't matter. How can you betray everyone you know by associating with a servant? It's nothing short of disgusting, if you ask me."

"And I'm sure plenty of your friends have sought your opinion."

"Indeed, and they don't think too highly of you." She crossed her arms with even more resignation.

"I will have to live with their poor opinion. Once Becca is returned safely to me, I am determined we shall wed as early as this spring."

Hazel wagged her finger. "You are making a fool of yourself, Nash Abercrombie." She let her voice linger on his last name, reminding him of its significance in society.

Nash was eager to move on to more important matters. "Did you say you have a missive for me?"

"I do. It contains a demand. A demand I think you will find distressing." She drew a letter out of her pocket. "You'll see it's a ransom note, asking the sum of three thousand for my return. But as you can see, I have not been kidnapped."

"Here. Give me that." Nash didn't intend rudeness, but he snatched the letter from her in a bold manner and read it.

Mr. Gill:

I no yur responsybal for Nash Abercomby's intinded, Hazel Calwell. We hav her hear saf and sownd and now we want the sume of $3,000 for her return. Met me at the Baptist

Metin Howse at 8 oclok tonit with the mony or else. Do not bring anybody else or yu wil regret it.

"These demands are terrible," Nash murmured.

"Indeed." Hazel watched him read, regarding him with a hint of satisfaction. "I wonder what they'll think when they find out they have a little match girl instead of a woman of substance?"

Nash rolled the letter in his hands without concentrating. "I doubt they'll care, as long as they get their money."

"Funny how they didn't recognize the little Hanham girl. You'd think they'd live right next door to each other."

"Just because her family is poor doesn't make them criminals. I resent that implication."

"I didn't mean such an implication," Hazel assured him, although Nash knew better than to believe her.

"At least this note means she's alive. My poor, gentle little Becca. I hope they are treating you well," he muttered, then looked heavenward. "I thank Thee, Lord, for such favor."

"Why I do believe you mean that?" Hazel observed. "No one will ever understand how you can love a little match girl when you could have married me, one of the most well-connected women in all of Providence. I'll certainly never comprehend how you could release me. When you first introduced me to your little maid, I was willing to fight for you. In fact, I had every intention of doing everything I could to ruin you. But no more. My sister and brother-in-law tried to convince me that you are worthy only of my pity and certainly unworthy of my time. Now that we have had this little meeting, I can see they are right."

Such a proclamation didn't surprise him. Mitchell's business dealings were aligned with his, so Nash's ruination—assuming Hazel possessed such power—wouldn't benefit their family. "I'm sorry to lose your good opinion of me," he said and meant it. "However, I deserve no less. Perhaps we can be on better terms in the future."

"Of course I will always be civil to you in polite society, Mr. Abercrombie, but my interests will lie elsewhere. I assure you, suitors will stand in line at my door as soon as they find I am free."

Not sure how to respond, he smiled. "I wish you well."

A slight pout visited her lips, a gesture she always used when upset and one he would not miss. He couldn't recall ever seeing Becca pout. "My relatives will not pay the ransom, so this problem is yours now." Triumph colored Hazel's voice. "By the by, according to the note, you have exactly five hours from now to pay. You'd better hurry."

"Five hours?" His stomach lurched. "Then I suppose I should thank you for bringing this letter to my attention."

"Of course. I wish you the best of luck. I don't approve of your taste, but it is not my wish to see even that little fortune seeker die at the hands of a kidnapper."

"Becca is not a fortune seeker, and if you insult her ever again, I shall never forgive you."

"Perhaps not." She gave Nash a sly look. "Although, I must speak now for your own good. For even though you have thrown me aside, I will always harbor a certain regard for you. Have you ever considered that she might know her captor?"

"No! I must protest—"

"Hear me out. Did you ever consider that, if not Becca herself, perhaps someone in her family might be setting up a ruse to collect money from you?"

He felt himself pale. "I—I hadn't considered such a thing."

"Perhaps you'd better consider it. Good day."

As Hazel left, Nash tried to put her suggestion out of his mind. Surely no one in Becca's family would stage such an event to extort money. Becca's observations about how her father treated her—treated all of their family—cluttered his mind. A drunk looking for his own benefit. But what would he have to gain? Wouldn't his future father-in-law be much better off allowing his daughter to marry him, affording her lifelong wealth instead of a one-time windfall? The story of the goose that laid the golden egg came to mind.

Nash couldn't help but focus on the note scrawled in a childish hand. "Lord, please forgive me for putting Becca in danger, even though that was never my intent. Guide me now, please."

He almost wished Becca's family had set up the kidnapping. Then he would know for certain she'd be safe. But if they hadn't, then the love of his life faced real trouble. If harm did befall her, he could never forgive himself. If only they'd chosen another day to go to the milliner's, Becca would be sitting beside him now, perhaps chattering about her new hats or making plans for the wedding.

Plans. God has a plan for everything, even if it's beyond human comprehension. He had to remember that. In the meantime, gathering the money to pay the ransom took precedence over everything else.

At that moment, he decided to refuse to consider the possibility of Mr. Hanham's involvement in the kidnapping. Nash would treat him as a worried father. He resolved to let his future father-in-law know about Becca's whereabouts. Perhaps Mr. Hanham would accompany Nash on the drive, although, fearing for his future in-law's safety, he would not allow him to meet the robber.

Glancing at the floor clock visible from its position in the dining room, he realized he had just enough time to go by the bank to collect his money, then see Mr. Hanham before he contacted the robber at the historic meetinghouse. He imagined the founder of the congregation, Roger Williams, would be none too pleased if he knew the site had been chosen for such a transaction.

Sitting alone in a small, sparse room, Becca prayed for help, recited the Lord's Prayer many times, and brought to her mind many Bible verses that gave her comfort. When would help come? " 'The Lord is my shepherd; I shall not want. He maketh me to lie down in green pastures: he leadeth me beside the still waters. He restoreth my soul: he leadeth me in the paths of righteousness for his name's sake. Yea, though I walk through the valley of the shadow of death, I will fear no evil: for thou art with me; thy rod and thy staff they comfort me.'"

The blond, whom Becca had learned went by the name of Maizie, entered without knocking. "Here's your dinner."

Becca's head snapped toward Maizie in surprise. Thinking of escape, she hadn't considered a meal. As much as she hated to admit it, the broth with carrots and corn preserved from the summer crop emitted an aroma that promised a delicious respite. A thin slice of coarse bread without benefit of fruit preserves accompanied the soup, along with a small cup of water. "Thank you."

She set the meal on the only table in the room and studied her charge. "What were you mumblin' to yourself?"

"A psalm."

"Oh." She shrugged. "Do you really believe all that rubbish they talk about in church?"

"Rubbish?" The idea of her Lord's Word being called "rubbish" offended Becca, but she didn't want to bristle lest she set off Maizie's temper and diminish her circumstances. "I—I believe in the Lord, yes."

"Lots of good that's doin' you now."

Becca paused. "The Bible didn't promise things would always be perfect, but He sustains me through hard times. I can tell you that."

"Is that so?" Maizie's mouth twisted in doubt.

Becca studied her captor, noting her unenergetic demeanor and sour expression. Against her will, she blurted a thought. "Are you happy?"

Maizie's mouth dropped open. "Happy? Why, I'd never thought much about it."

Becca didn't see how anybody could be happy living with criminals and taking part in their crooked way of making a living, but she decided that wasn't the time to pass judgment. "Well, I'm happy most of the time, even though life for me isn't perfect. My faith helps me."

"Then you must be the only person in church who's not a hypocrite."

Becca noticed the hurt in the woman's eyes. "I'm sorry someone disappointed you. But not everyone will. May I pray for you?"

She gasped, and for the first time since Becca saw her, a hint of a smile shone on Maizie's face. "For me? You'd pray for me? You don't have reason to do that." She paused and narrowed her eyes. "Wait. This is a trick. You want me to help you escape, don't you?"

"I'd like that," Becca admitted, "but that has nothing to do with my prayers for you. I'll pray for you right now. We can pray together."

She startled. "Y–you're the first person what ever offered to do that for me."

"Then let's pray now—"

"Maizie!" her companion called from the next room. "What's the matter?" She entered the room. "Is the girl givin' you trouble?"

"No. No." She shook her head in quick motions, then turned her face to Becca. "I'll be back to pick up your dishes shortly."

Though the opportunity to pray with Maizie alone was lost, Becca said a prayer that the Lord would keep her in

His care and guide her to a better life walking with Him. She petitioned that another opportunity to pray with Maizie would present itself and that in the future God would put more sincere Christians in Maizie's path. Then, in a soft voice, she said a blessing and ate the meal in silence. The delay meant lukewarm soup, but the broth comforted her even as anxiety never left. At least since she had shown compliance, they had chosen to trust her enough not to bind her or stuff her mouth to keep her quiet. For those kindnesses, she was thankful. Yet she longed to see the one sure to be her rescuer.

Nash, where are you?

❧

Calculating that he had just enough time, Nash went about his business quickly, deciding to be driven in his carriage rather than riding on horseback in case Mr. Hanham did agree to accompany him to rescue his daughter. Nash first stopped by the bank. The institution's president scratched his head and looked at Nash with doubting eyes when he withdrew such a large sum. Though innocent, Nash felt guilty. Thankfully no one questioned him. With the money in his pocket, he instructed Jack to drive him to Mr. Hanham's.

"Stay here and wait, Jack," Nash instructed as he disembarked.

"Yes, sir."

Nash hoped the driver would obey. Jack had become even more careless of late. Glancing at the sidewalk, Nash noticed stares coming his way and wondered if Becca felt odd when she arrived in such style each evening.

Becca. He prayed he'd see her soon.

Nash remembered the day he asked Mr. Hanham for Becca's hand and had spent considerable time with the family. Would he ever become accustomed to such poverty? The conditions still shocked him. Looking around, Nash tried not to show his disdain. The homes had never been fine, but neglect hadn't helped. Nash realized that in most cases, lack of money rather than sloth resulted in their unkempt appearance.

Children wearing rags walked about with no shoes. Their image reminded him of Becca that long-ago night when her eyes beckoned him to help her. He'd never regret that, no matter what happened in the future.

He knocked on the door.

"Who is it?" yelled Mrs. Hanham.

"Nash Abercrombie."

"Nash! Nash!" some of the children cried before opening the door. Becca's two-year-old brother and three-year-old sister ran to him and hugged his legs. He greeted them and smiled for the first time since Becca was kidnapped. The older girls, hovering in the background, looked at him with awe as though he were some kind of angel.

Their mother turned to them. "Girls, be on yer way."

"But, Mother—"

"Be on yer way." At the sound of her raised voice, the small child she held started yelping, and she rocked him on her hip. "Mr. Abercrombie, nice to see ya. To what do I owe this pleasure?"

He doffed his hat. "I wish this were a social call. The matter I have on my mind is quite urgent. May I speak with your husband?"

Her mouth dropped. "I'm sorry. I ain't got no idea where he is. Is everythin' fine?"

He wished he could console her, but to do so would be to lie. "If I may ask, you have no idea when he might return?"

"No, sir."

Nash couldn't help but wonder if Becca's father was with the criminals, just waiting for him to appear at the meeting-house with the money. Anger flared at the thought, and he prayed it wasn't so. "And you have no idea where he's gone?"

She shook her head. "I don't have fine tea, but ya can come inside for a spot of ale. I'm sure my husband wouldn't mind if

I give ya some under the circumstances."

"Forgive me for being unable to accept your hospitality, but I must take leave of you."

"Is—is everythin' all right?" she asked again.

Nash searched for something comforting to say but could offer little. "I pray it will be in due time. I'll be back."

Without time to search every tavern in town for Becca's father, Nash found Jack waiting for him. He sighed with relief and instructed him to drive to the meetinghouse. As Nash rode, his nerves jangled, but he had to face his enemy. Unwilling to put his driver in danger, he disembarked two blocks before the meetinghouse.

"If I don't return in half an hour, summon the police."

"I don't think it's right for me to let you go alone, sir. Let me come with you."

"I can honestly say I wish I could, but the letter said I am to bring no one. I wouldn't dare put you in danger by doing so."

Jack nodded slowly. "Yes, sir. I'll be right here."

Twilight was falling, so the trees cast ominous shadows. He set his chin high and walked like a brave man to the meetinghouse.

"Stop right there," a voice commanded from the shadows. "Don't get smart. Remember the gun? I still have it, and if I have to shoot, this time I won't miss."

twelve

Nash walked toward the sound of the harsh voice coming from behind the meetinghouse. "I won't try anything. I'm unarmed."

A man emerged, holding a gun on Nash.

Nash recognized him as the robber he saw earlier. He displayed his hands, fingers spread, to show he spoke the truth. "Please, put your weapon away. I don't seek to harm you. I only want Miss Hanham back." He put his arms down but kept his hands in full view of the robber as he looked for Becca. "Where is she? I won't give you any money until I see her."

"That's yer mistake. I'll give ya the girl when I'm ready." Still holding the gun, the robber studied him. "Say, ye're the man what was with Miss Caldwell when this whole thing started."

"That's right. Only you don't have Miss Caldwell in captivity. You have Miss Becca Hanham. My fiancée. I am Nash Abercrombie."

His eyes squinted in confusion. "I don't know what ye're talkin' about." He scowled. "This better not be a dirty trick."

"It is not." Nash lifted his hands another inch for emphasis.

"Well, I don't guess I care who ya are, as long as you got my money. Do ya?"

"Yes, I do." He patted his suit coat to indicate its location.

The robber nodded and inspected the horizon. "Are ya alone?"

"Yes. I would never endanger anyone about whom I care." *At least not intentionally*. He swallowed. "So where is she?"

"You'll see her. For now, I want the money. Hand it over."

154

He shook the gun at Nash to show he meant business.

"All right then." Nash withdrew a roll of large bills and threw it near the man's feet. Even in the darkness, he could see the greed in the kidnapper's eyes as he hurried to retrieve the money.

For the first time, the man's gun wasn't pointed at Nash. Taking advantage of his distracted condition, Nash charged him. With a quick chop of his wrist, he knocked the weapon from the man's hand. He followed the movement with a knee to his soft belly. The man fell to the ground. Nash recalled his boyhood days of playing cricket and with agility retrieved the weapon lying nearby before his adversary could beat him. Though the criminal weighed more than Nash, he was strong enough to hold him in a vise grip with his hands and knees. He put the Colt revolver's barrel to his temple.

"No! Don't shoot me!" The kidnapper's arms shook as he held them upward on the ground to signify surrender.

"Where is she?" Nash's voice sounded threatening even to his own ears. "I demand to know."

He shook his head. "I don't know. My partner said he'll send word where to meet her tomorrow."

"That's not good enough." Seeking to fortify his advantage, Nash retrieved the money from the ground, then pressed his knees deep into the man's inner thigh. "And you are in no position to tell a falsehood."

Sweat beaded on his brow, and he grimaced. "I said I don't know."

Nash exerted so much pressure on the man's leg that he could feel sinewy muscle under layers of fat. He could smell the stench of nervous perspiration. "I'm the one with the gun now."

The man grunted, and his face became even sweatier. "All right. I'll take you to her, but only if you give me half the money now."

Nash tried to conceal his anger at the man's gall. "I won't

even consider giving you anything until I see her."

He cut his gaze sideways in the direction of the gun and scowled. "Fine. Come with me."

"Don't try to escape." Nash rose to his feet. He never allowed the gun's barrel to point away from the man's head.

Huffing, the man used considerable effort to steady himself. He rubbed his thigh where Nash's knee had bruised it and scowled at his captor.

"It's not as amusing to be the one held with a gun to your head, now is it?" Nash couldn't resist asking without an ounce of levity.

His frown deepened.

"I'm concealing this gun in my coat pocket, but it will continue to be pointed at you at all times," Nash warned. "Do not even think about making a false or sudden move."

The man nodded.

"I'm going to lead you to my carriage now." Jack would be waiting since nowhere near a half hour had passed. The idea that Jack would help him keep the robber under control relieved Nash. He swished the gun eastward. "Take the path. My driver is waiting."

"I told you not to bring anybody," he growled.

"That is neither here nor there now. Go."

Nash could feel anger emanating from his captive, but he obeyed. After all, only a fool would argue with a revolver.

They kept walking along the path, well past where Nash had been certain he'd left Jack waiting.

"How much longer?" the robber asked. "My leg hurts."

Nash tightened his lips. How could he admit to this criminal that he couldn't depend on his own driver? Normally Nash wouldn't employ someone so unreliable. Often he wished his father had never promised Jack's mother they'd take care of her boy. To leave Nash alone in the dark, knowing he was to meet an armed man—the thought upset him. Still, Nash had to maintain his composure.

"We'll keep walking," Nash ordered. "Lead me to her."

"I don't know if I can with this bum leg," he protested.

Nash drew the gun from his pocket so its full force would come into view. "You can and you will."

"Oh, all right," the man growled.

Nash put the gun back in his pocket. They walked toward Brown University on College Hill. He feared an accomplice might pounce on him, but no such event occurred. Instead, well before they reached the school, the robber ducked into a brick house. A lone light shone through a front window.

Nash's heart beat wildly as they stepped over the threshold. Joy at the prospect of seeing Becca battled with sickening images of his beloved bound and gagged. He listened for muffled cries of distress coming from anywhere in the house.

Nash was surprised when a woman greeted them rather than another man. Surely this plain and plump member of the fairer sex wasn't a criminal. But anyone who held his beloved Becca for ransom couldn't be held blameless.

"Is this Mr. Gill?" Though not a conceited man, Nash caught a flirtatious inflection in her voice.

"No, it's Mr. Abercrombie. The girl's fiancé."

"Oh." Disappointment colored her voice. "So, what—what did you bring him fer?"

The robber's eyes narrowed. "Shut up, woman. That's not yer concern."

Another woman, a blond, entered. "What's going on in here?"

"Where is Miss Hanham?" Nash tilted his head toward the door from which the blond had appeared. "Is she in there?" He restrained himself from pushing past her and finding out for himself.

The woman ignored Nash and addressed her comrade. "Did he give ya the money?"

"I will give you the money when I see Miss Hanham," Nash snapped. "Where is she?"

"Miss Hanham? Who is that? I've got Miss Caldwell with me." The plump woman looked to the robber for guidance. "Dolph, what is the meaning of this?"

"Quiet. I'll explain later. Show him to the room."

She looked puzzled but obeyed. "Come with me."

Nash watched as the woman unlocked the door of a back room. With only one candle for light, Becca sat in a chair. To his relief, they hadn't placed her in restraints. Nash pushed past the woman and ran to his beloved. "Becca!"

She gasped, jumped up, and ran into his arms. "Nash! I've never been happier to see you!"

"Nor I, you." He squeezed her in the way of a fond protector before breaking their embrace. He looked into her eyes. "Did they treat you well?"

Becca's glance went to her captors and back. "As well as a kidnapping victim can be, I suppose."

"You've retained your sense of humor, I see." He smiled at her. He wanted to cover her face with kisses, but since others were present, he refrained.

Dolph's rough voice interrupted his dream state. "Well, ain't that nice?"

Nash turned his head to see him holding a gun on them. He felt himself flush with embarrassment. How could he have been so careless? Allowing himself to become distracted, he had put them in danger. He reached in his pocket for the weapon he had confiscated from his opponent.

"Don't even think about it," he said. "Put your hands up and come along with me."

"I'm sorry, Becca," he muttered into her hair.

"God is with us." Her courageous assurance defied the fear he saw in her eyes.

"Is that what you think?" Dolph sneered. "Then ya'd better

say yer prayers since ya ain't got much time left. Now hand over the gun and the money, or I'll take both of 'em from ya."

Seeing no alternative, Nash surrendered to his demands.

Dolph took the roll of bills and handed it to his companion. "Put this under the bed." She nodded with quick jerking motions.

"Don't you worry none," he assured his companion. "I'll be back for you."

ꝏ

Becca couldn't remember when a walk through town took so long. Under cloak of darkness, the kidnappers had changed locations from the cottage in the woods just in case someone tipped off the law. She could feel her pulse in her throat. She could tell by the strained look on Nash's face—which she could see since her eyes had adjusted to the lack of light—that he was hatching a plan for escape. She prayed he would be successful.

"Stop." The man's abrupt command forced them to obey. Becca nearly ran into Nash as both of them came to a halt.

A buggy awaited them on Olive Street. In such a conveyance, commonplace all over town, no one would ever guess its passengers were being held captive. The criminals had thought of every way to keep from being discovered, as far as Becca could see. What would happen to Nash and her now? Her heart beat fast as her fear increased. Was this the night she would die? Though confident she would see the loving face of Jesus when the Lord called her home, Becca nevertheless wanted to live long enough to marry Nash and give him a family. Such prospects seemed more and more slim as their time with the robber increased.

Holding a silver flask, the thin man they called Mac jumped from the driver's seat. "What took so long?" he snarled, revealing a missing front tooth.

"Don't worry. Everything went just as planned."

Nash stared at him.

"Well, almost. I got the man—well, the man what cared enough to pay the ransom. And I got the girl and the money, just as we said. What more do ya want?"

Becca wanted to cry out, to do something, anything, to get out of the situation. What did Nash want her to do? She sent him an imploring look, but he shook his head almost indiscernibly, signaling her to remain calm. Standing with his usual perfect posture, she wondered how he could retain such composure.

If the kidnappers had any idea what Becca was thinking, they didn't let on. Dolph curled his fingers at his partner, asking for the flask. He extended a fleshy hand. "Here, give me a swig o' that. It's been a long night, and I need a snout full."

"There ain't much left." Mac relinquished the refreshment.

Dolph drank deeply and then wiped his mouth with his sleeve. He tilted the open flask toward Nash. Becca smelled the bitter odor of whiskey but didn't flinch since she was accustomed to the stench, thanks to her father's habits.

"I don't care for any, thank you," Nash responded with more politeness than the situation warranted.

"I wouldn't be so picky if I was ye," Dolph said. "Ya might not like the plain old corn liquor I got. Ye're used to fancy French wine, I'll wager."

Despite his goading, Nash stood erect, and his expression didn't waver.

"Whatever you take now will be your last." He waved the flask in front of Nash's nose.

"That's right." Mac laughed. He eyed Becca, his thin face reminding her of a scarecrow. "I notice the girl didn't even bat an eye when she smelled our liquor. I thought society women turned up their noses at our humble beverages. Mebbe she drinks in secret. Mebbe she'd like a swallow." He leaned toward her. "How's about it, girl?"

Dolph protested. "What? I wouldn't waste my liquor on any woman. Well, mebbe one or two o' the wenches I know at the tavern, when I wants to put 'em in a good mood." He winked, and Becca shuddered. She felt Nash's body tense even though they weren't close enough to touch one another.

The men pushed them into the buggy, which was soon on its way. She didn't wonder why they didn't bother to blindfold Nash and her. They had no plans for them to see the light of day again. To Becca, each second in time seemed to be an hour. Finally they came to a stop.

Dolph got out but held his body near the exit. "Get out."

She obeyed and surveyed the location. The place Dolph had forced them to halt was so remote and forested that Becca knew screams would never be heard. She envisioned Dolph digging a shallow grave for their dead bodies and running off with Nash's money. She studied the revolver. At least if he shot them, their deaths would be quick.

"Heavenly Father, save us!" Becca prayed aloud as her foot sank into muddy ground.

Dolph and Mac laughed in tipsy mirth. "She thinks God will help her now. I get tired of hearin' her pray. Don't ye?" Dolph nudged Nash with a force that made Becca jump.

"Never." Nash pursed his lips, but the glint in his eyes gave Becca courage.

"Turn around," Mac demanded.

"So you're going to shoot us in the back. I might know men such as yourselves wouldn't have the courage to face us in our moment of death." Nash's voice sounded harsh.

Moment of death? How could he be so calm? Yet he was every bit the man. The strong man she loved. The man with whom she wanted to spend the rest of her life.

If we die tonight, I will have gotten that wish. I will have spent the rest of my life with him.

Becca's breathing had become pronounced. Couldn't he

take this chance to grab the gun? What did they have to lose? Death was certain if he didn't do anything, but a bit less certain if he did. "Nash, please!"

The men chortled. "There's nothin' he can do fer ya now," Mac insisted.

"That's right," Dolph agreed. "Men like him, they look down on people like us. For once, we got the upper hand."

"And if ya want ta know the truth, I'm havin' me a bit o' fun with it all," Mac admitted.

The smile on Dolph's face looked nothing short of evil. "Ya were brave before, knockin' the gun out o' me hand, but I was alone then. Ya wouldn't dare try anything like that, with it bein' both of us. And if ya do, things will be worse for yer girl here."

Too fearful to be ashamed by making a pleading gesture, Becca sent Nash the most puppy-eyed look she could muster, begging him to do something, anything. His glance went back and forth between the two men. Surely he was thinking. . . .

Without warning, Nash let out a whoop that could have awakened the dead and gave Mac a swift kick. In a flash he followed suit with Dolph. "Run, Becca!"

Becca wanted to remain and kick and punch the criminals as well, but she imagined her little blows wouldn't accomplish much. Besides, if she ran fast enough, perhaps she could find help.

She wished she didn't have to run from the scene in spite of realizing that was her best course of action. Desperately she wanted to know Nash would survive, yet to sacrifice her life when he had just done so much to save her would dishonor him. She rushed into the darkness. "Lord, I beg Thee to help us!"

The sound of a horse's hooves beating on the path shocked her. Who could be out this time of night and in such a remote place? She stopped and looked at the path, then back at Nash. Dolph punched him in the gut while Mac held him.

Tears streaming down her face, Becca's stomach churned, but as soon as the criminals heard the horse, they stopped beating Nash. Widened eyes told her they didn't know how to react. They hadn't expected anyone to ruin their plans. Becca was sure the horseman must have witnessed what he interrupted. Anticipating the stranger would keep her safe, Becca ran back toward the scene.

The rider drew close enough to be heard. "Stop! Stop right this instant!"

Becca's hand clutched her throat when she recognized the sharp baritone. So uncertain was she that her voice quivered. "Father? Father, is that you?" How could it be, when they didn't own a horse?

As soon as she uttered the words, the criminals panicked. One fired a shot at the horseman.

Becca's hands shook as she sent them skyward. She screamed, "Father!"

Having escaped injury, Father jumped off the animal and ran toward the group. Dolph lifted his gun to shoot, but Nash charged him. Grabbing his opponent's wrist, Nash was able to keep the gun from hitting its mark. Meanwhile, Father subdued a hapless and drunken Mac.

Becca feared they wouldn't be able to keep the men under control long. In answer to silent prayer, she heard the sound of approaching horses.

"That's the police," Father told Dolph. "After me wife told me you stopped by, I summoned 'em before I came here."

Nash and her father kept the criminals confined long enough for the police to arrive and take charge. After the police expressed their gratitude to Nash and her father for their bravery, they departed.

Becca hugged her father. "Thank you, Father! Thank you from the bottom of my heart."

His mouth twisted in an unusual show of modesty.

"Father, I never guessed you would be my rescuer. Why, you were shot at, all for me. I can't believe you would make such a sacrifice."

Nash agreed. "Thank you, Mr. Hanham. If you hadn't appeared the moment you did, I'm not sure what the outcome would have been. I don't think I exaggerate when I say I owe you my life. I cannot express my gratefulness enough."

"You can express it by takin' care o' me daughter."

"Father!"

Nash laughed. "That's quite all right, Becca. I intend to take care of you anyway. I can only hope our next trip to the milliner's won't prove so dramatic."

Becca sent him a rueful smile. "Perhaps next time she can deliver the hats to our house."

ಶಿ

"There you are!" Mother's face relaxed with relief as Nash, Becca, and Father entered the noisy front room. "I was so worried. What happened?"

"Tell us! Tell us!" Naomi added amid the siblings' pleas to hear about the adventure.

Father filled them in on the evening's events. To Becca's surprise, he didn't exaggerate. Then again, they had such a close call that stretching the truth hardly seemed necessary.

"How terrible! Let me look at ya." Mother did just that. "Oh, I'm so relieved ye're safe and sound!"

"As am I," Nash agreed. "But tell me, how did your husband know where we were?"

"Let me tell it," Father said. "Yer driver, Jack, was at the pub. I could tell by the way he was braggin' in front o' me that he didn't recognize me. But I sure recognized him. He was sayin' that he was comin' into some big money soon."

"Wait, you say Jack was at the pub? Tonight?" Nash's voice registered his surprise, then his disappointment.

Mr. Hanham nodded. "He said he had a couple o' men collectin' money fer him, but he'd be a rich man in a matter of hours."

"Then no wonder he wasn't there when I needed him," Nash muttered, hurt evident in his voice. "He abandoned me deliberately."

Father didn't seem to hear Nash. "Bein' a man o' the world as I am, I decided I'd better figger out what Jack meant. I figgered he wouldn't talk without a few drinks, so I engaged him in talkin', tellin' him he must be smart, and by plyin' him with ale. It took awhile, but I finally got him to the place where he said he had a girl out in the woods near the old cemetery who was mighty valuable. I didn't understand exactly what he meant, but I knew somebody was in danger. Then he said luck was with him and his friends. Without plannin' it, they kidnapped his employer's fiancée, and that gave 'em the chance to ask for a ransom. When he said that, I knew I had to do somethin' fast."

Becca held back a gasp.

"I ran home, not even finishin' me ale, mind ya. I went to the smithy and gave him the promise of a dollar to let me borrow his horse so I could follow you, Mr. Abercrombie. He wouldn't a let me have it, 'cept I told him ye're a rich man and ye'd make good on it." He paused and stared at Nash. "Ya will, won't ya?"

Nash smiled. "Considering I came out of our adventure with the full amount of money and my life—plus the life of the only woman I've ever loved. . ." The look he sent Becca said it all. "I'd say I'd be happy to give the smithy ten times as much."

"A dollar's enough." Father lifted his index finger to hold their attention. "I don't pray much, but I did ask God fer some help tonight. I suspect I should give Him credit fer me spyin' a buggy makin' its way down a road out of town.

'Mighty odd time fer anybody to be headin' out o' town,' I thought to meself. So I follered it. But I was thinkin' with me brain, I was." He tapped his temple. "Before I left town completely I thought to ask a little boy sellin' lucifers on a street corner to tell the police to go in the same direction the buggy was goin', 'cause there might be trouble brewin'. I paid him a penny. He seemed happy enough."

Nash nodded. "I'm glad they took the boy seriously. But then again, they've been desperate to capture this band of thieves, so no doubt they were following up on any clue."

"Thank goodness they were finally successful," Becca noted. "I was going to run as fast as I could to find help, but I was so afraid I would never see Nash alive again." She placed a hand on his arm. "Oh, Nash, you were so brave!"

"With the Lord as my guide." Nash looked at Becca's father. "I'm thankful for your quick thinking, Mr. Hanham. My driver has some explaining to do. To the police."

Becca felt sorry for Jack, but he had brought his punishment on himself.

Nash's expression turned wistful. "The Lord used another unlikely person to help us. If I'm to be honest, I must say that I have Hazel to thank as well."

"Hazel?" Becca asked. "That is strange."

"Yes. She's the one who showed me the ransom note sent to her brother-in-law. That told me right away I needed to act quickly." He sighed. "That was before I let the criminals know I am engaged to you, not Hazel."

Becca smiled, blushing.

"I propose a big celebration, a formal party for all our friends. At that time we shall announce our engagement and wedding date."

"Are you sure?" Becca asked.

"More sure than ever." The conviction in his voice did more than enough to convince her.

"But Miss Caldwell. . ."

"I assure you, she has no reason to hope for our match any longer."

"Oh." Becca faced him straight on and looked him in the eyes. Eyes she wanted to see every day for the rest of her life. "You kept up your end of the bargain. I don't remember a time I've been happier. But I know I was not born to your world. To marry me will be a sacrifice for you. I want you to know that from this moment, I release you of any obligation you feel toward me. I want you to feel free to marry a woman of your own station. That's what my dream is for you—acceptance by your friends and your happiness."

"If you really mean that, then you'll marry me tomorrow. Your spirit touched me that night long ago when I first bought lucifers from you, but when I saw you again as a beautiful young woman, my heart was captured. The time we've spent together since then has only confirmed my initial feelings for you. Now I can't imagine life without you." He sent her a boyish grin. "If you'll marry me, I promise you'll never have to touch another dirty dish." He lifted her left hand in his and regarded the ruby ring. "Grandmother instructed me to give her ring to my future wife. When I presented it to you, I meant to keep my promise. I don't want a society maiden. I want you, Becca Hanham. If you'll have me."

"If I'll have you? Why, I'd marry you even if you lived right here on this street."

Laughing, Nash took her in his arms. They kissed, knowing their time together had bonded them forevermore.

epilogue

Nash and Becca stood under an ivy-covered archway leading to the gardens of the Abercrombie country estate a few miles from Providence. The delicate scent of flowers gave the air the feel of a wedding. A four-tiered cake Cook took two days to bake and frost graced the center of a buffet table.

Becca looked up into Nash's eyes. "I have married the man I love today."

"You only love me today?" Nash teased, holding his arm around her waist. "But I will love you today, tomorrow, and every tomorrow God sees fit to grant us, my darling."

"As it shall be. My love for you will never die."

Becca wouldn't have cared if they'd married in a barn, but the wedding itself had been everything she could have imagined and more. She looked out among their guests as they indulged in the wedding feast held outdoors under a lovely New England summer day. They had all wished her well as Mrs. Nash Abercrombie. Even Hazel, now being courted by a wealthy older man, didn't seem to begrudge her such happiness.

She couldn't help but notice Father looking stiff in formal wear and her brothers pulling now and again on their collars, but her male relatives had all done her proud by displaying their best behavior. Even the smaller siblings, acting as ring bearer and flower girls, shone. Mother and Becca's sisters blossomed in the environment, reminding Becca of the rose petals their guests had placed along the garden path for Nash and her.

During the engagement period, Becca had come to know

his intimate friends and had even drummed up the courage to perform for them. After she sang her initial song, the others joined in and had great fun showing off their respective talents to one another. Many such a pleasant night of music and parlor games bonded them, so her fears that they would never accept her had long since faded. Clearly their high regard for Nash superseded any urge toward snobbery. Then again, Nash had trained her well, and she felt more and more comfortable among his set as time progressed. The idea of socializing with them for the rest of her life no longer seemed formidable. Nash did confess that his friends had quieted a few snippets of gossip, but that only proved their loyalty. Two of Nash's customers dropped their accounts with him to protest his match with Becca, but the Lord quickly sent more to replace them. Truly, the Savior had answered their prayers in every respect.

Nash surveyed the buzzing reception along with her. "I understand we have one of the largest wedding parties reported in Providence."

Becca laughed. "When one has so many siblings, that's likely to happen. And look at Mother and Father. They are absolutely beaming."

"I hope they'll enjoy their new home. There should be more room for all your siblings now. Granted, they will still share bedchambers with one another."

"Yes, but in quarters not nearly as cramped," Becca was quick to point out. "I'm so grateful to you. For the first time in my memory, Father has stopped drinking, and my brothers and sisters aren't spending their time daydreaming about how to leave home as quickly as they can. I'm so glad they'll be living near us, too. I couldn't ask for more."

"I wouldn't have it any other way."

"What a dream." Becca sighed. "To have everyone I love near me always—especially you, Nash. I never considered being well-off or powerful, and certainly I never envisioned that I would be a member of your society. I never thought I'd wear anything but rags, and here I am in the finest garments I can imagine. Yet none of those things matter to me." She looked into his face, marveling once again at how handsome he looked. "The dream you have made come true for me is one of undying love. The love of a compassionate man of God was all I ever wanted. Thank you for giving me that."

"The gift of your love has made all my dreams come true, Becca. I'll love you forever."

Unashamed of their love, they shared a kiss, the first of the many more they were assured of sharing for the rest of their lives.

A Letter To Our Readers

Dear Reader:
In order that we might better contribute to your reading enjoyment, we would appreciate your taking a few minutes to respond to the following questions. We welcome your comments and read each form and letter we receive. When completed, please return to the following:

Fiction Editor
Heartsong Presents
PO Box 719
Uhrichsville, Ohio 44683

1. Did you enjoy reading *The Master's Match* by Tamela Hancock Murray?
   ❏ Very much! I would like to see more books by this author!
   ❏ Moderately. I would have enjoyed it more if

   _____

   _____

   _____

2. Are you a member of **Heartsong Presents**? ❏ Yes ❏ No
   If no, where did you purchase this book? _____

   _____

3. How would you rate, on a scale from 1 (poor) to 5 (superior), the cover design? _____

4. On a scale from 1 (poor) to 10 (superior), please rate the following elements.

   ____ Heroine   ____ Plot
   ____ Hero   ____ Inspirational theme
   ____ Setting   ____ Secondary characters

5. These characters were special because? _____
   _____
   _____

6. How has this book inspired your life? _____
   _____
   _____

7. What settings would you like to see covered in future
   Heartsong Presents books? _____
   _____
   _____

8. What are some inspirational themes you would like to see
   treated in future books? _____
   _____
   _____

9. Would you be interested in reading other **Heartsong
   Presents** titles? ❏ Yes ❏ No

10. Please check your age range:
       ❏ Under 18   ❏ 18-24
       ❏ 25-34   ❏ 35-45
       ❏ 46-55   ❏ Over 55

Name _____
Occupation _____
Address _____
City, State, Zip _____

Presents

♡

HEARTSONG
PRESENTS

If you love Christian romance…

$10.⁹⁹

You'll love Heartsong Presents' inspiring and faith-filled romances by today's very best Christian authors…Wanda E. Brunstetter, Mary Connealy, Susan Page Davis, Cathy Marie Hake, and Joyce Livingston, to mention a few!

When you join Heartsong Presents, you'll enjoy four brand-new, mass-market, 176-page books—two contemporary and two historical—that will build you up in your faith when you discover God's role in every relationship you read about!

Mass Market 176 Pages

Imagine…four new romances every four weeks—with men and women like you who long to meet the one God has chosen as the love of their lives…all for the low price of $10.99 postpaid.

To join, simply visit www.heartsong presents.com or complete the coupon below and mail it to the address provided.

✂ -

YES! Sign me up for Heart♥ng!

NEW MEMBERSHIPS WILL BE SHIPPED IMMEDIATELY!
Send no money now. We'll bill you only $10.99 postpaid with your first shipment of four books. Or for faster action, call 1-740-922-7280.

NAME _____

ADDRESS_____

CITY_____ STATE _____ ZIP _____

MAIL TO: HEARTSONG PRESENTS, P.O. Box 721, Uhrichsville, Ohio 44683
or sign up at WWW.HEARTSONGPRESENTS.COM